THE LOST BUCKAROO

THE LOST BUCKAROO

Bliss Lomax

GUNSMOKE

First published in the UK by World's Work

This hardback edition 2011
by AudioGO Ltd
by arrangement with
Golden West Literary Agency

ISBN 978 1 445 85679 7

British Library Cataloguing in Publication Data available.

Printed and bound in Great Britain by
MPG Books Group Limited

Bliss Lomax was a pseudonym for **Harry Sinclair Drago**, born in 1888 in Toledo, Ohio. Drago quit Toledo University to become a reporter for the Toledo *Bee*. He later turned to writing fiction with *Suzanna: A Romance Of Early California*, published by Macauley in 1922. In 1927 he was in Hollywood, writing screenplays for Tom Mix and Buck Jones. In 1932 he went East, settling in White Plains, New York, where he concentrated on writing Western fiction for the magazine market, above all for Street & Smith's *Western Story Magazine*, to which he had contributed fiction as early as 1922. Many of his novels, written under the pseudonyms Bliss Lomax and Will Ermine, were serialised prior to book publication in magazines. Some of the best of these were also made into films. The Bliss Lomax titles *Colt Comrades* (Doubleday, Doran, 1939) and *The Leather Burners* (Doubleday, Doran, 1940) were filmed as superior entries in the Hopalong Cassidy series with William Boyd, *Colt Comrades* (United Artists, 1943) and *Leather Burners* (United Artists, 1943). At his best Drago wrote Western stories that are tightly plotted with engaging characters, and often it is suspense that comprises their pulse and dramatic pacing.

THE LOST BUCKAROO

List of Chapters—

The Lost Buckaroo

Chapter One

THE FABULOUS MINE

PROFESSIONALLY AND SENTIMENTALLY, Rainbow and
Grumpy had long since come to regard Reno as the
crossroads of the West. The town was like a magnet, draw-
ing men from half a dozen states, good men and bad and
all the shades in between, mining men, stockmen and a rare
assortment of flamboyant characters who fitted into no
definite category. Reno was wide-open, alive, big even in
its littleness, and once the tinsel of its divorcée colony
and the trappings put on for the tourists were torn away,
Western from its toes to its finger tips. It explained why
so many business transactions were consummated there
that could have been handled just as well in San Francisco or Salt Lake City.

Whenever an opportunity presented itself for them to
spend a few days there, the partners never failed to take
advantage of it. They had been in Nevada for almost a
month this time, having been called in by the authorities
at Star City in connection with the mysterious slaying of
Henry Jennifer, the well-known and immensely wealthy
cattle king. Having brought that matter to a successful
conclusion, they were in Reno now, on their way home to
Wyoming.

This was their last evening in town. Stepping out of
the elevator at the Golden Hotel a few minutes after six,
and already late for a dinner engagement, they got only

halfway across the lobby when a redheaded young man jumped up from his chair and gave them a hearty greeting. He was Asa Workman, the district attorney at Black Rock.

Though they had not met in several years, the famous pair readily remembered the able young prosecutor.

"It's good to see you boys again," said Workman. "We often speak about you in Black Rock. We haven't forgotten how you cleaned up that ring of killers and claim jumpers for us. I see your names in the newspapers from time to time. Seems you clicked again at Star City."

Rainbow nodded and said, "We had some help. An old friend from Black Rock, by the way. Or maybe I should say a friend from our days in Black Rock, since she makes her home in California."

Workman showed his surprise. "I know you must be referring to Miss Seng, the young Chinese woman who is held in such high esteem by her people. Surprising that your paths should cross again."

"It ain't the first time," Grumpy informed him. "She's most likely to bob up when we need her most." The little man glanced at his watch. "We ought to be gittin' along, Rip."

"I'm sorry I kept you," Workman said apologetically. "If you're going to be in town a day or two, I'd like to have a talk with you."

"We're leaving for Wyoming at midnight," Rainbow told him. "Professor Greenwood, of the Mackay School of Mines, and his daughter have asked us up to the house for dinner and to spend the evening. It'll be late when we get back. I'm sorry we can't get together this time."

"That's all right, Rip. You and Grumpy run along. And remember me to the professor. He was teaching geol-

ogy when I was attending the university. That was before
the Mackays gave the U. of N. the School of Mines. Have
you known him long?"

"For years," said Rainbow. "We've often turned to
Henry Greenwood for expert information when we've
been on a mining case."

The partners hurried out. Hailing a public carriage,
they gave the driver the Greenwood address on upper
Sierra Street.

Workman returned to his chair and the friend with
whom he had been chatting. Like himself, his friend,
Dennis McCaffery by name, was a district attorney from
Wolf River. Their counties adjoined, and they were in
Reno, prior to going to Carson City to argue a tax matter
before the State Supreme Court.

"That was Rainbow Ripley and Grumpy Gibbs, the
famous detectives," said Workman. "Rip is the tall one.
You've heard of them, of course."

"Naturally. Ripley is still a young man. His pint-size
partner is getting along in years, isn't he?"

"Don't let that fool you," said Workman. "Little
George Gibbs is a shrewd rooster and as tough as bullhide.
They make a great pair, Dinny. They're expensive, and
they demand a free hand when they're called in. But they
get results. They still like to call themselves range detectives. I suppose that's the cowboy in 'em. As a matter of
fact, they haven't taken a rustling case in years; they got
beyond that a long time ago. If you ever find yourself up
against something you can't handle, I can recommend
them to you."

McCaffery smiled.

"I don't believe we'll be needing their services. We've
got a sheriff who's on his toes, and a marshal who sees to

it that the town doesn't get away from him. With between three and four hundred men employed in the mines and smelter on Midas Mountain, you know Wolf River isn't the sleepy little cow town it used to be. It's a riot at times; but we don't try to keep the lid on too tight."

"That's decent of you." Workman laughed heartily, and it was heavily on the sarcastic side. "You couldn't do anything else if you tried! It would be bad for business. I know how that goes. A town will stand for a lot when cash money is rolling in."

"Yeah," McCaffery agreed. "That's about the size of it. Nobody gets excited over a few broken heads and a little bloodletting, if it's between friends. We'll even stand for an occasional homicide." His blue eyes twinkled. "Sam Clemens (Mark Twain) hit the nail on the head when he was a young reporter on the *Territorial Enterprise*. He said no one need worry about crime till it began to appear in the headlines."

The two of them laughed together.

"I'll knock on wood when I say it," McCaffery added, "but I don't think we'll have any reason to send for your friend Ripley and his partner."

It was a conversation that the Wolf River prosecutor was to recall with peculiar interest some months later. For Rainbow and Grumpy, it was an evening that was to stick in their minds, too. Experience had taught them that seemingly trivial and, at the time, widely unrelated matters had a surprising habit of suddenly becoming important and often developing a strange continuity. And yet, as they sat in the living-room with Greenwood and his daughter Lane, listening with interest to the former's tales of his desert wanderings that engaged him every summer, it never occurred to them that what Professor

Greenwood was saying would one day be remembered as something more than an entertaining narrative.

Though he was an expert geologist and had a scientific knowledge of minerals and mining, Henry Greenwood was a confirmed desert rat. For years he had been trudging up and down and across the Great Ralston Desert and the sprawling wastelands of Nye County, an area larger than most Eastern states. A few days after the university closed for the summer, accompanied by Moy Kim, the huge Chinese who had cooked and served the dinner they had eaten this evening, he would disappear from Reno and not be back until the fall semester was about to get under way. He had found gold several times, but never in quantity.

Lack of success had not dimmed hope in him nor dulled the eager light in his eyes, for he had the fanaticism of the true gold seeker. It had kept him young. He was a thin, wiry man, who certainly didn't look his fifty-five years.

He spoke of the Lost Buckaroo, which had engaged his attention for the past three summers.

"I know I'll find it some day," he declared quietly. "It's down there somewhere below Toquima Basin, between the Monitors and the Solomon Mountains. If I've accomplished nothing else these past three years, I've narrowed the hunt down to an area of fifty square miles, more or less."

"That's still a lot of country if a man has to go over it with a fine-tooth comb," Rainbow observed.

"Yes and no, Rip. Most of it will eliminate itself at a glance. That old saw about gold being where you find it is a myth; any competent geologist can say to a certainty where you won't find it. Prospecting an unexplored region isn't so difficult if you use a scientific approach.

There're so many things to help you. You can study the strata and the faults and the composition of the base rocks. If it doesn't look good to me, I move on. I'm absolutely confident I haven't left the Lost Buckaroo behind me."

"I shore would like to take a flyer on somethin' like that, with a man who knows what he's doin'," Grumpy remarked. He had been following every word with absorbed attention. Years ago, he had been severely bitten by the gold bug and he had never gotten over it.

"But tell me this, Greenwood," he continued. "What makes you so shore this Lost Buckaroo ain't jest another one of them cock-and-bull stories that have had men scratchin' all over this state for fifty years?"

The question elicited a merry laugh from Lane Greenwood. Her dark eyes flashed a mischievous smile at her father.

"I can give you the reason for Dad's scratching, Mr. Gibbs. It's an old story with us; I've had to explain it a thousand times. I'm sure that behind our backs most people say we're a little cracked, but the story of the Lost Buckaroo grows on you, and I believe every word of it. One of these days we Greenwoods will show all the doubting Thomases how wrong they were."

"There you are, gentlemen!" her father exclaimed happily. "With someone rooting for me like that, I wouldn't dare to think of giving up."

Rainbow realized that the professor and his daughter were very close to each other. Lane was an only child, and with the passing of her mother she had become her father's housekeeper as well as secretary. At twenty, she was a very attractive young woman, with a sensitive, intelligent-looking face. Her wide mouth and strong chin gave

her face character and indicated that she had a will of
her own.

It was Rip's opinion that she had more sense than one
usually found in a girl of her age.

"I'll begin with the familiar 'Once upon a time,' Mr.
Gibbs," said Lane, "when the Wolf River district was
cow country. There was a buckaroo by the name of Johnnie Bidwell working on the Taylor Brothers' ranch. He
was considered a rather worthless character, because he
wasted whatever spare time he could find in prospecting
for gold."

"There's been a hundred like him, myself included!"
Grumpy volunteered. "Gold fever has ruined more cow-
punchers than whisky and wimmen put together."

"Well, anyway, along comes Andrew McCray and makes
his big strike on Midas Mountain," Lane continued. "It
turned everything topsy-turvy around Wolf River. Johnnie Bidwell gave up his buckarooing, bought himself a
prospecting-outfit, and set out to find his fortune. There's
some question about how long he was gone, but before
the summer was over he was back in Wolf River, claiming
he had made a rich find, and he had some samples of
gold to prove it. He didn't register his claim nor would
he even hint as to where his find was located. He was
afraid the property would be jumped if he made legal
entry of the ground. He wanted a new outfit and a couple
of partners who could hold the fort while he came back a
second time to file."

"I bet he didn't have no trouble gittin' someone to
throw in with him," the little man declared. "Show up
with a fistful of rich ore an' it's jest as easy as stringin'
fish to git men to believe you got a big gold mine jest the
other side of nowheres."

Lane glanced at him in mock reproof. Grumpy caught it.

"Don't git me wrong, honey!" he protested quickly. "I ain't sayin' yore Johnnie Bidwell was runnin' a windy on them folks. I was jest thinkin' back to an experience or two of my own. You go on with yore story. Who'd he git to throw in with him?"

"Ab Foraker, the hardware merchant, and William Bigelow, the hotel proprietor. They outfitted, and after Johnnie had spread it around that he'd kill the man who attempted to follow them, they managed to leave Wolf River unobserved. They were gone a long time. And then one day the three of them returned; Johnnie Bidwell had been unable to find his way back to his mine. For five or six years, he tried again and again to locate it, until no one would grubstake him any longer. Others tried to find it, too, and they failed. Most of those old-timers are long since dead and buried, and the Lost Buckaroo has become just a legend to everyone but Dad and me and Perce Robbins, an old assayer in Wolf River."

"I suppose a violent sandstorm is the explanation," said Rainbow. "Johnnie Bidwell must have found an exposed stringer of rotten quartz with some rich values and picked out his samples. Before he got back, drifting sand could have covered it and changed the whole look of the country."

Greenwood shook his head.

"You're wrong, Rip. Those samples were not hacked out of dead quartz; they came from a vein in live rock. They were chipped off as clean as you please. If you were to go to Wolf River today, you could see them in Perce Robbins's place. He keeps them locked up under glass, along with a lot of other specimens. I've studied them by the hour. I know the type of formation they came from. That's why I'm so confident I shall be the one to find the Lost Buckaroo."

"It isn't much to go on," the tall man argued.

"It's enough for me," Greenwood insisted. "I'm a confirmed unbeliever in most of these tales about so-called 'lost' mines; but I can't laugh off those samples Johnnie Bidwell brought in. They're as real as the furniture in this room. He'd made a real strike, all right. In his excitement, he lost his bearings completely. That's the only explanation I can give you. I went into the Toquima Basin from Austin, the first two years. Last year, I started in from Eureka. I would have been surprised, indeed, if I had found anything. All I was doing was narrowing down the field. It'll be different this summer. I'll outfit in Wolf River, and I'll be out to hit the jackpot this time."

They continued to talk about the Lost Buckaroo until Rainbow and Grumpy were ready to leave.

"Wal, Henry, you know we wish you the best of luck," the little one said, as he shook Greenwood's hand. "But tell me this, what'll you do with the mine if you find it?"

"I won't do a blessed thing until I know I can protect it. I don't propose to find it only to have it stolen away from me."

Rainbow gave him a shrewd glance.

"That sounds as though you thought you might run into trouble."

Greenwood shrugged.

"I wouldn't say that, Rip. We've got some blacklegs in Nevada who'll try anything if the stake is big enough and they think they can get away with it. Knowing it, I'll keep my eyes open, if I have any luck."

The partners reached the sidewalk and started to walk

back to town. As they passed the low hedge that separated the Greenwood yard from the one next door Grumpy suddenly darted into some shrubbery and pounced on a man concealed there.

"By hickory, I thought I saw you go over that hedge!" the little man rapped. "Git to yore feet and give an account of yoreself or I'll tap you on the head with my gun!"

"Please!" the stranger pleaded. "Don't make a disturbance, Mr. Gibbs! I can explain everything to you and Mr. Ripley."

He got to his feet and proved to be a young man of clean-cut appearance, possibly twenty or twenty-one years of age.

"Can we walk down the street a short distance so we won't alarm the Greenwoods?" the young man asked.

"Okay," said Rainbow, surprised that the stranger knew their names. Getting a good look at the youngster's face, he doubted that the boy was a sneak thief.

Half a block from the Greenwood house, they stopped.

"Go on, talk!" Grumpy growled.

"I'm Del Blanchard, a senior at the university," the young man began. "I expect to get my degree as a mining engineer in June. I'm very fond of the Greenwoods. I guess you might say I'm Lane's beau. I'm at the house three or four nights a week. Lane told me you gentlemen were coming to dinner, so I didn't show up this evening."

"You were on the porch, listening to what we were saying, weren't you?" Rainbow demanded, still trying to get to the bottom of the incident.

"I was on the porch, but I wasn't listening to what was being said," Blanchard replied. "I've heard Professor Greenwood talk about the Lost Buckaroo for hours.

There's nothing about it I don't know."

"Then what was the idea of jumpin' over the hedge and hidin' out like that?" Grumpy snapped.

"I didn't want to be caught on the porch. I knew I'd have to explain to Lane and her father. I didn't want to do it. I thought it might alarm them."

"What do you mean by that?" Rainbow inquired. He gave the little one a glance. "Let the boy tell his story, Grump."

"Why, last night, sir, I saw two men loitering in front of the Greenwoods', when I came along about eight o'clock. They didn't see me; I was cutting across this vacant lot. It's a short cut I often use. The two men weren't hoboes; they were well dressed. They passed the house once and then turned and came back. It was a warm evening, like it is tonight. The windows were open. I could hear Lane calling to her father."

"Wal, go on!" Grumpy urged.

"I dropped down in the weeds when I realized they were going to pass within a few feet of me. They went by as I lay there. I couldn't see their faces. I thought they might come back. I waited, but I didn't see any more of them. I decided not to say anything to Lane or her father. I figured I'd better be sure I knew what I was talking about before I said anything."

"You thought they were planning to break into the house, of course," said Rip.

"I thought of that, but I didn't give it much consideration, sir; I figured it was something else. You'll laugh, perhaps, but I thought it might have something to do with Professor Greenwood's plans for this summer. He's never made any secret of his interest in the Lost Buckaroo; his talk is always just as unguarded as it was tonight.

I know most people will tell you there never was such a mine. But there are a number of people who believe it just as much as he does, and they're pretty well agreed that if it's ever found, he'll be the one to find it."

Rip nodded. He found himself liking young Blanchard.

"I think I understand you," he said. "You mean that someone may have got the idea that if they knew exactly what the professor's plans were they could beat him to the punch, or lay back and let him lead them to the mine."

"Exactly, sir. That's why I spent this evening watching for them."

"You saw them again?" Rainbow questioned.

"Yes, sir. They stopped in front of the house while one of them filled and lighted his pipe. He took a long time doing it. Your voices carried to the sidewalk. I knew they were catching everything you said, so I slid off the porch and started for them. They saw me coming and they started walking at once. I followed them up to the corner. They turned over to Lake Street and headed back to town. I haven't seen anything of them since."

"Huh!" Grumpy snorted disgustedly. "That wa'n't no way to handle things. If yo're goin' to play detective, son, you better take some lessons. How did you know what you was walkin' into? The sensible thing for you to have done was to tip us off."

"Just a minute, Grump," Rainbow interjected. "The boy thought he was doing the right thing. I'd have liked to fire a question or two at those men. As it stands now, we don't know whether there's anything to this or not. Chances are there isn't. Their business might have been entirely innocent."

"I don't know about that," the little one objected.

"Looks mighty suspicious to me. I say, let's go back and have a talk with Greenwood. We've got time. If it doesn't do anything else, it'll make him a little more cautious."

"I don't think it's necessary for us to go back," said Ripley. "Blanchard can accomplish more than we can." He turned to the latter. "You make it your business to see Miss Greenwood in the morning. I'd put my cards on the table with her if I were you. You can tell her you spoke to us and that it's our opinion that she should go to work on her father and insist that he keep his plans to himself. It can't do any harm, and if, by chance, some-one is interested in getting a line on him, that'll stop them. You understand?"

Del said that he did.

"I'll see Lane after my first class in the morning."

The partners picked up their bags at the Golden and went over to the depot. The following morning they were rolling through eastern Nevada. After breakfast they wandered back to the observation car, where Grumpy managed to find a map of the state.

After studying it for a few minutes, he said, "I can lo-cate the town of Wolf River, all right, but there ain't no stream of water indicated on the map. Have you ever been in that country, Rip?"

"Once, years ago. The river is just a big wash with a tiny creek running through it. It's an arid, treeless coun-try, and they get some bad cloudbursts. I was told that the wash really boils over two or three times a year." He smiled indulgently. "You still dreaming about the Lost Buckaroo?"

"I shore am," the little man acknowledged. "I can't git Greenwood's story out of my mind, nor what hap-pened last evenin'."

"You better," Rainbow advised. "We've got a job to do for Wells Fargo and we better be thinking about it. Henry Greenwood will have an enjoyable summer and be back in Reno late in September, and the rainbow he's chasing will be as far away as ever. If he gets fun out of it, that's enough. I don't know why you should be stewing about it; it doesn't concern us."

Grumpy screwed his grizzled face into a frown. "I don't know about that," he muttered soberly.

Rip grinned.

"Don't tell me you've got a hunch."

"I don't care what you call it!" the little one growled, stung by Rainbow's bantering. "By hickory, you could be wrong for once, and this might be the time! I got a feelin' in my bones that we ain't heard the last of the Lost Buckaroo!"

Chapter Two

PHONY PROSPECTORS

RAINBOW AND GRUMPY had been gone from Reno for a week when Cordell Blanton came up from Tonopah and established himself at a small hotel on Virginia Street.

Cord was no stranger in Reno. In fact, there were few places in the state where he didn't feel perfectly at home. For a dozen years and more he had never failed to put in an appearance whenever a new gold camp sprang into existence. Over the years, he had come to be regarded as a rather prominent figure in Nevada's floating population. His professions were many. He had been gambler, hotel proprietor, saloonkeeper, dance-hall impresario, and, of late, owner of Goldfield's most popular eatery.

Though he had turned some sharp corners in his time, his reputation had not suffered noticeably, and in the free-and-easy world in which he circulated, he was generally regarded as a square shooter.

He was a Southerner, a Carolinian, he said. His manners and appearance bore it out. A tall, rangy man, with good teeth and a smile to show them off, he carefully avoided being a dandy. It was a conscious restraint with him and, along with it, he managed an air of detachment that few ever pierced. It enabled him to keep an eye on the future and contemplate the plans of other men. It was not strange, therefore, that Henry Greenwood's pursuit of the Lost Buckaroo had attracted his attention.

The vaporings of ignorant desert rats, and he knew a hundred of them, fell on deaf ears whenever he was importuned to supply the necessary grubstake. Great riches had been promised him so often he had lost track of the mythical fortunes he had tossed away by refusing to open his purse strings. Other men, more gullible than he, had availed themselves of these missed opportunities, but it was not of record that they had ever reaped any reward.

It had confirmed Blanton in his cynicism. And yet he was a confirmed gambler at heart, and gold was a magic word to him. In various ways he kept himself well-informed regarding the trends and fluctuations of mining operations throughout the state. From the pages of mining news that appeared in all Nevada newspapers, he plucked the gossip and optimistic speculation that was as unfailingly bright with promise as a desert sunrise. It not only enabled him to keep track of the professor's comings and goings, but provided many stray bits of information concerning Greenwood. Indeed, the latter would have been flattered, not to say alarmed, had he known how interested his activities had become to Blanton.

Cord had convinced himself that Henry Greenwood was something more than an overeducated ignoramus, teaching geology and metallurgy to a bunch of kids but knowing nothing about practical mining. Proof of it was to be found in the fact that the big mining companies often called him in as a special consultant, when their own engineers ran into difficulties. He was, Cord told himself, a man who might reasonably be presumed to know what he was doing; it passed belief that he would go methodically about finding a lost mine, spending summer after summer at it, unless he had some secret knowledge regarding it.

It could only mean that the Lost Buckaroo actually existed.

Blanton was as convinced of it as Greenwood himself. He was not only prepared to do something about it, but had already taken the first step. The mysterious strangers who had aroused Del Blanchard's suspicions were Blanton's men, and he was in Reno to discover what they had learned. Since he was expected, they got together with him a few minutes after he reached his room.

"Cleve and me was lookin' for you yesterday, Cord," the older of the two remarked, settling himself on the bed. He was a stocky, sandy-haired man, apparently in his late forties. His name was Pat McGarry. He had known hard work in his time, and his huge hands still bore signs of it. "I thought you said you'd be up on Tuesday."

"I did, Pat. Something came up. Did you and Cleve get a line on him?"

"We sure did," the younger of the two answered. "And we damn near stubbed our toes, too. We started hanging around his house in the evening, figuring if we could sneak up to a window we might get an earful. The young punk who runs around with Greenwood's daughter spotted us after we'd been up there a couple nights. We tried it once more and we almost got in over our heads." Cleve Miller chuckled over the near mishap; he had worked for Cord, off and on, in various capacities, for a number of years and knew how to stand up to him. "Greenwood had company. Who do you think was there?"

Blanton shook his head; he wasn't in Reno to be amused or answer riddles.

"Rainbow Ripley and his partner, the detectives. Don't dead-pan me that way, Cord! You know who they are.

They're the gents that put the rope around Mike Mc-
Queen's neck in Black Rock and sent Speed Daggett up
from Nevada City to his little necktie party in the prison
yard at Carson. Remember 'em now?"

Blanton tried to frown him down.

"You're a pain in the neck when you try to be funny.
I know all about that pair. Did you and Pat have a run-in
with them?"

"No, no! Nothing of the kind. They never laid eyes on
us."

Blanton breathed easier.

"You had me worried. Are they getting ready to go to
work for Greenwood?"

"No, just old friends of his. They're back in Wyoming
by now."

"Yeah?" Blanton queried skeptically.

"That's right, Cord," McGarry spoke up. "They was
out here on that Jennifer killin' and just stopped over on
their way East."

In Pat's book, Blanton was always the headman, and
he showed him a deference he never got from Cleve Miller.

"Greenwood tells everybody his business," McGarry
continued. "Findin' out what we wanted to know wasn't
much of a trick. Cleve can tell you."

Cord glanced at Cleve. It was meant as an invitation
for him to begin. With infuriating nonchalance, the latter flipped a cigarette into shape and took his time about
lighting it. Cord watched him with narrowed gaze, prom-
ising himself that he'd put Miller in his place one of
these days.

"Well," he rapped, "whenever you get ready!"

Cleve grinned, but his lean, deeply lined face lost none

of its hardness. He enjoyed goading Blanton to fits of anger. Having accomplished his purpose, he tossed away his cigarette and was suddenly ready to talk.

"He's going in from Wolf River this year," he said. "He figures on pulling away from there about the twenty-fifth of June. The big Chink's going in with him, as usual."

"Where's he heading for?" Blanton asked.

"There's some sort of a ranch on a place called Calamity Creek. He's going to fill up his canteens there and jump off for Toquima Basin."

"He was all over the basin last summer," said Blanton. "That can't be it."

"Course it ain't. He's going right through the basin and down into the Solomons. On the level, Cord, Greenwood's so cocksure of himself he's told some folks he can draw a ring around fifty square miles of that country down there and have the Lost Buckaroo inside it."

"That's right, Cord," McGarry chimed in, when he saw the doubt in Blanton's eyes. "Both of us got it from different parties. And he's goin' purty far down the Solomons, too, or he wouldn't be sayin' he can allus depend on Spanish Tanks for water. I know Spanish Tanks. They ain't the only springs down there, but the others lie south of Spanish Tanks."

Pat was the only one of the three who had had any practical experience as a prospector and miner. He was a hardrock man and had been a mucker and driller, and finally the assistant superintendent of the rich little Henrietta Extension, in the Bullfrog district. This last had been his undoing, for he had made the rather common error of cutting himself in as a silent partner for the owners. The law caught up with him presently and took him out of circulation for upward of three years. Incarceration had not sharpened his wits nor removed the larceny from his soul, but his luck had been better of late, with Blanton to tell him what to do.

Cord was pleased with what he had heard, even though he refused to get excited. From McGarry and Miller he drew little details regarding Greenwood that they considered unimportant. Many of them were unimportant, but he wanted the whole picture.

"Seems we got something definite to work on," he acknowledged at last. He eyed the open transom. "Get up and close it," he told Cleve, "and I'll tell you what we're going to do."

Miller not only closed the transom but opened the door and glanced around the hall, making sure no one had been eavesdropping. For good measure, he turned the key in the lock.

"Listen, Cord," he said thinly, pulling his chair a little closer, "we ain't going into this half-cocked; we're going to think it out before we do anything."

"I'll take care of that end of it," Blanton informed him bluntly. "I got it all thought out. Either one of you known in Wolf River?"

"I never saw the place in my life," Cleve answered.

"And you, Pat?"

McGarry said no.

"Good!" Cord exclaimed. "You say Greenwood plans to shove off about the twenty-fifth of June. I want you boys to show up there about the twentieth. That'll give us all the time we need. I'll hit town a couple days ahead of you. I'll give out that I'm in Wolf River looking things over with the idea of opening a saloon and restaurant. I'll run into men who've been in my place in Tonopah. I know they got nothing like it in Wolf River. When it gets noised around that I sold out and may open up there, it'll set me in right. When you boys bump into me, we're to be strangers, understand?"

"What's the idea of that?" asked Cleve.

"I'll tell you—and get this straight. You and Pat are going to take yourselves down to Sodaville, buy a couple burros and a prospecting-outfit. Don't say nothing about the Lost Buckaroo. If anyone mentions it, laugh it off. You got other plans, see? You're shoving off for the Solomons and up into Toquima Basin. Stick to that story, no matter what comes up."

"Dammit, Cord, that's tough country!" Cleve protested vehemently. "We don't know it; we can get lost!"

"Pat knows it," Blanton corrected. "Do as he says and you won't get lost."

He turned to McGarry.

"Pat, you can find Spanish Tanks without any trouble, can't you?"

"Sure. We can be there about five days after we pull away from Sodaville."

"Okay!" said Cord. "You don't have to hurry. Spend a day or two around the Tanks and act like you was really trying to locate something good. You may see some Chinks in there, looking for gold; they savvy that desert country, and they'll stick with anything they find, even if it don't mean no more than wages. They won't bother you; just don't have no truck with them."

"This is a swell party you're rigging up for us!" Cleve Miller complained. "Why do we stall around the Tanks for a couple days?"

"Because I want your story to be airtight!" Cord's tone was sharp with irritation. "If you'll shut up, I'll tell you what your story is going to be!" He addressed himself to

McGarry. "When you leave the Tanks, Pat, head north into the basin. There's no water in Toquima Basin, they say. You'll have to pack enough to last you ten days, when you pull away from the Tanks. I don't believe it'll take you that long to reach Wolf River, but you want to play it safe. We'll get a map this evening and try to figure things out as well as we can, so we can settle on the day you're to leave Sodaville."

"We don't spend no more time in the basin than we have to?" McGarry asked.

"No, keep right on moving. You've already made a discovery down in the Solomons, understand? And you're heading into Wolf River, looking for somebody with cash money to throw in with you."

"In Wolf River we can sell a bill of goods to Cord Blanton, the man with the cash money," Cleve observed, a mocking note riding his tone.

"That's the idea!" Blanton snapped. "You'll come to me, and you'll find me hard to interest. You'll need some ore samples. You ought to be able to put your hands on some, Pat."

"That'll be easy," McGarry told him. "Greenwood oughta be showin' up in Wolf River a couple days after we git in. We don't pay no attention to him, I figger."

"That's right," Blanton agreed. There were times when McGarry seemed to have more brains than Cleve, he thought. "You're too excited about your own find to give a damn about what Greenwood does. I make a deal with you boys. We won't make any secret about it; the more who know, the better. We'll outfit and get away as soon as we can."

"You mean we'll pull out before Greenwood leaves Wolf River?" The question came from Miller, and the way it was put said plainly enough that he didn't approve.

"Sure!" Cord retorted. "That's the only sensible way to play it. We'll lay out in the basin and let him pass us. With a good pair of binoculars, we can keep cases on him without him getting wise. We'll pack in grub enough so we can stay out a month. If this takes longer than I figure it will, one of us can come back for fresh supplies. If any questions are asked about Greenwood, our story will be that we haven't seen anything of him."

That took care of everything as far as Blanton was concerned. He caught Cleve Miller regarding him coolly and unimpressed.

"You ain't finished, Cord," Miller challenged. "There's a couple other details. When—and if—Greenwood locates the Lost Buckaroo, then what?"

Blanton's face whitened angrily; he had stood enough of Cleve's badgering.

"What's eating you, Miller?" he growled. "You know what we're after and what we'll have to do to get it. We agreed on that a long time ago. Greenwood won't be the first man to lose himself in that country and never be heard of again."

"That part of it is all right with me," Cleve retorted. "But this ain't no taffy pull we're talking about. The desert's got a damned nasty habit of giving up its secrets, and you know it as well as I do. If we get tagged with this business, all three of us will be jerked to Jesus. Let's use our heads a little and keep as far away from Wolf River as we can. We can get into the Solomons and lay out for Greenwood without letting every punk and his brother in Nevada know what we're up to."

"No! You're dead wrong!" Blanton's face had whipped

hard and flat. He'd had enough of this bickering; he was footing the bills and things were going to be done his way. "Get sneaky about this and we'll trip ourselves, sure as hell! Somebody would be sure to remember something. Little things would be put together, and the first thing we knew, we'd be nailed. If you want to be suspected, just try to cover up. That'll do it every time!"

Cord's teeth flashed forbiddingly. He wasn't through.

"We'll play it wide-open," he said decisively. "That'll leave us an out, no matter what happens."

"Yeah!" McGarry agreed solemnly. "That's how it's goin' to be. And we won't have no more arguments about it."

His round little eyes fastened on Cleve belligerently.

"Okay! Okay!" the latter said flippantly. "A guy's got a right to say what he thinks, ain't he? I just wanted to be convinced. My neck won't be the only one that'll get stretched if this thing backfires. Keep that in mind. It's after six. Do we eat?"

"You and Pat get your supper somewhere," Blanton answered. "I'll eat by myself. The three of us don't want to be seen together in Reno."

Such prudence delighted Cleve.

"I like that, Cord. You *are* playing this close to your vest, sure enough."

Blanton smiled enigmatically.

"That's the way I aim to play it, Cleve. As you said, we've got to use our heads a little."

Chapter Three

WELL-ACTED SCENE

TOM STEWART, THE ROTUND MAYOR of Wolf River, had an office over the Excelsior Hose and Engine Company fire house. He was seldom there, however, a comfortable chair in the lobby of the old Union House giving him a far more sociably desirable headquarters from which to manage the affairs of the town. By custom, his chair was reserved for him, and he could usually be found there, or at the hotel's bar, a few steps to the rear.

He was there this morning, in his shirt sleeves, as usual, a rakish panatela clamped between his teeth, when Cord Blanton came in. He waved Cord over and invited him to sit down.

Blanton had been in town several days and had given out that his avowed purpose in Wolf River was to open an establishment comparable with the popular bar and grill he had operated in Tonopah. He had correctly surmised that the news would be received with interest.

No one had given the idea a more enthusiastic reception than the mayor. The town had its share of saloons and restaurants, such as they were. But they were not to be mentioned in the same breath with the mirrrored palaces of food and drink to be found in booming Tonopah and Goldfield. A place of that sort, Tom proclaimed, was what Wolf River needed to let the rest of Nevada know that its current prosperity wasn't just a flash in the pan.

"How does it look, Mr. Blanton?" he inquired. "Are you goin' to be able to talk turkey with someone?"

"I don't know," said Cord. "There's a couple places that could be made over into what I want. But when you start talking terms, the price goes right through the roof."

"There's some good unimproved property on the street," Stewart observed. "You could build."

"I've given that some thought. I don't want to build; it would be months before I could open up. But I might come to it. In any case, I'm not going to be in a hurry, I've got a little vacation coming to me. As far as Wolf River goes, I'm thoroughly sold on it. It's bound to grow."

"It can't help it, Blanton!" Tom declared positively. Lowering his voice, he said, "If you'll keep it under your hat for a few days, I'll let you in on a little secret. We're goin' to have a standard-gauge railroad from Wolf River to the Espee main line before snow flies. They'll make the announcement and begin replacin' the narrow-gauge as soon as the material can be brought in."

Cord voiced his interest, and it was not altogether feigned. He had seen enough to realize that the town held an opportunity for him. In fact, he had begun to tell himself that if the reckless adventure on which he had embarked panned out successfully the best thing he could do would be to give Wolf River a resplendent emporium of food and drink, such as he had been talking about.

The profit to be garnered from such a venture was a secondary consideration with him. Once the secret of the Lost Buckaroo was his, he wanted to be situated where he would be in a position to protect it. Wolf River would serve his purpose better than any other town.

Blanton's plans for the mine ran far beyond anything he had discussed with Miller and McGarry, and for the perfectly valid reason that the latter did not figure in them. The two considered themselves his partners; but that was their mistake. They were only his tools; when they had served their purpose, there would be various ways in which they could be liquidated.

Cord continued to circulate around town, spending his money freely in the saloons, particularly in the Silver Dollar, Wolf River's most popular resort. He kept his conversation on the safe side, never permitting himself to be pinned down to anything definite.

Blanton extracted some amusement from it, especially with Russian Louie, the proprietor of the Silver Dollar. The giant Slav had amassed a comfortable fortune in his eighteen years in the States and wanted to return to his native Smolensk. He had exhibited pictures of a smiling *ninotchka*, who, he claimed, was waiting for him. Cord had heard the tale and knew Louie was secretly anxious to sell, despite his vehement protestations to the contrary. Buying the Silver Dollar became a game of cat and mouse between them. Blanton could have named a compromising figure and purchased it half a dozen times a day, if he had been so inclined.

Apparently, Cord had nothing troubling him as he lolled around Wolf River. That wasn't the case at all; Cleve and Pat were already overdue. So many things could have happened to them that he couldn't name a reason and be satisfied that he had guessed correctly.

Another two days passed without bringing them. Blanton's detachment and reserve were not equal to it. In his mounting anxiety he easily convinced himself that they were in trouble. He damned them for fools and bunglers as he paced the floor of his room in the Union House.

"They either got lost or ran out of water!" he raged. "Lay out every step for them—tell 'em exactly what to do—and still they could mess everything up for me!"

That was all that mattered to Blanton; they had brought all his scheming to naught. He wasn't concerned about whatever bitter fate might have overtaken Cleve and Pat.

All morning and most of the afternoon Cord remained locked in his room, plunged in the depths of despair. This enterprise wasn't something he had turned to on the spur of the moment; he had been months putting it together. Every move had been carefully thought out. It meant exactly nothing now. The stupidity of a couple of half-wits had ruined everything. You couldn't pick up the scattered pieces of such a plan and come up with a satisfactory substitute.

"I wouldn't trust it if I could," he brooded. "I'd need time, and I haven't got it; Greenwood will be showing up in a day or two. I can kiss the Lost Buckaroo good-by right now!"

It took him some time to condition himself to that fact. His interest in Wolf River was gone.

"To hell with it!" he growled. "I won't stick around here! When the train pulls out for the north in the morning, I'll be on it!"

He shaved and managed to pull himself together, after a fashion, before he went downstairs. Tom Stewart was in his chair. Cord had no time for him; he was through with that nonsense.

At the hotel bar, he found consolation and courage in some excellent bourbon. Things might be worse, he conceded; his plans had gone awry but he was in the clear. He even tried to tell himself that Greenwood might not find the Lost Buckaroo. That was asking too much, and he put the thought out of his mind as though it were some rank heresy.

It was after five when he went up the street, his mouth set at a contemptuous angle. He needed a laugh, and the best place to find it was in the Silver Dollar, talking to Russian Louie.

Louie had a lingo all his own and a quaint sense of humor that was always on tap. Suspecting that Blanton had dropped in to talk business, he craftily shied away from saying anything even remotely concerned with the Silver Dollar and harked back to his younger days in Alaska.

Cord saw through the subterfuge and was mildly amused. He marveled, too, that a stupid ignoramus like big Louie, with his laughter that was like booming thunder, could come to this country penniless and put together possibly as much as forty to fifty thousand dollars in a few years.

From where they stood conversing over the bar, they could observe the flow of life along Wolf River's main street. Neither paid it any particular attention until Blanton was suddenly electrified to see a little cavalcade of two men and their burros plodding through the dust. Every step brought them nearer, until he knew he couldn't be mistaken. It was Cleve Miller and Pat McGarry! They were here! Everything was all right, after all! They had just miscalculated!

Cord wiped the excitement out of his eyes.

"What's that outfit, Louie?" he inquired, as the two men trudged past. "Friends of yours?"

Louie took a closer look.

"Nagh! Jus' some desert faller been out look for gold." Louie shook his head skeptically. "They not find him, I tank."

"Not likely," Cord agreed.

He bought another drink and then returned directly
to the hotel; he didn't want to encounter Miller and
McGarry before they had an opportunity to tell their
story to others.

The dining-room was open. Blanton went in at once
and was surprised to find he had an excellent appetite.
He took his time over supper. When he was finished, he
strolled out into the lobby and, finding a vacant chair,
settled down to enjoy a good cigar and keep an ear tuned
to the current of conversation going on about him. He
didn't have to wait long to catch the first reverberations
to the arrival of his lieutenants in Wolf River. Tom
Stewart came in. He had Dennis McCaffery, the district
attorney, with him. They sat down across from Blanton.
The latter was not acquainted with McCaffery but knew
him by sight.

"I don't know how important a find it is, Tom,"
McCaffery remarked, "but it isn't the usual hot air they're
handing out; they brought a bagful of samples in with
them. They've found something, all right."

"Good-lookin' ore?" Stewart inquired.

"I haven't seen it myself. Others have. Charlie How-
land, for one. Charlie says it's fairly rich-looking stuff."

"Wal, that's good!" Tom declared. "I hope they've
really got it. It wouldn't hurt Wolf River a bit." He
chuckled knowingly. "You got any idea where they made
their find?"

"Somewhere below the basin. They're not talking too
much, Tom. You can't blame them. They admit they're
just about flat broke. What they need now is someone
with some loose cash."

"That's usually the rub," the mayor observed. "Where
they hangin' out, Dennis?"

"Chris Stengel's feed barn. You're going to be around; you'll bump into them tonight. Let me know if you get anything out of them. I've got to be getting home; the missus has asked some people in to play cards this evening."

"Sure," Tom said. "Tell me, are you jest curious or have you got the itch to take a flyer on a proposition like this?"

McCaffery laughed.

"I don't know what I'd take a flyer with, Tom. I've got the new house to pay for. But a man can do a little dreaming, can't he?"

"Sure," Stewart said again.

Dennis left, and a few minutes later Tom waddled out of the hotel and disappeared up the street.

"It's perfect!" Cord said to himself. "It's working out just as I figured it would!"

In the course of the next hour, he overheard more talk in the same vein. It was as though he had dropped a stone in quiet waters and was sitting back, watching the circles widen.

Cord sauntered into the Silver Dollar a few minutes after nine. There was a crowd at the bar, and in the center of it stood Cleve and Pat. Tom Stewart was firing questions at them. He held a piece of gold-bearing quartz in his hand, which he continued to examine.

"How much of this stuff do you figger you got?" he asked.

"We don't know," Cleve answered for himself and McGarry. "There's no way of telling till we've had a chance to do some work."

"They may have found the Lost Buckaroo," a man at the bar declared. "Ask 'em, Tom."

Stewart communed with himself for a moment. "It could be the Lost Buckaroo," he declared. "You boys ever heard of Johnnie Bidwell and his Lost Buckaroo?"

"Not that I remember," Pat spoke up. "Where was it located?"

"Huh!" Tom snorted. "Nobody knows. It wouldn't have stayed lost if anyone knew. There's a man at the Mackay School of Mines who claims he can locate it, but he's been tryin' to do it for years and ain't got no results so far."

"Nobody'd ever been into this ledge before us," Pat said flatly. "We opened it up and found the vein. And I can tell you we took dang good care to cover it up before we left. We ain't registerin' no claims nor nuthin' of the sort; what we got is goin' to lay right where it is till we can git someone to come in with us who's got money enough to open up the property."

"That's right," Cleve chimed in. "We ain't interested in talking business with any tinhorn."

"You can't sell a pig in a poke," Stewart argued. "Nobody's goin' to throw in with you 'less you can show him somethin'."

"We'll show him plenty," said Cleve. "An assay will give him an idea of what we've got. When we're satisfied we got the right man interested, we'll take him in with us and let him size up the property. But we ain't taking that chance till we know who we're dealing with."

Blanton silently congratulated himself; his men were doing better than he had dared hope. He let the talk continue for a few minutes before he began to edge into the crowd. Cleve saw him, and then Pat. No flash of recognition passed between them.

When Stewart handed the sample back to Miller, Cord

THE LOST BUCKAROO 37

laid a hand on the mayor's arm.

"Tom, could I have a look at it?"

"I don't know why not, Blanton," was his chuckling answer. "We've all had a look at it."

Cord studied the specimen for a minute or two.

"Some values in it," he said. He passed the specimen to Cleve. "Looks good."

Cleve gave him a sharp, scrutinizing glance.

"Mister, ain't you from Tonopah?" he inquired. "Don't you run the Elite down there?"

"I used to," Cord answered with a smile. "I sold out a few weeks ago."

"I thought I wasn't mistaken," said Miller. "When this gentleman called you Blanton, I knew you was Cord Blanton, sure enough. Say, if you're looking around for something to put a little money in, why don't you let me and my partner talk to you?"

Cord dismissed the suggestion with a laugh.

"It wouldn't do you boys any good to talk to me. I hate to pass up a good thing, but I got other plans for my money."

"I reckon you'd change your mind if you knew more about our proposition," Cleve persisted, knowing that was what Cord expected of him. "What we need wouldn't begin to put a dent in your bankroll, Mr. Blanton. A few hundred dollars would cover the cost of the assay, some giant powder, and grub enough to last the three of us a month. You wouldn't have to put up any real dough till you had a look at the property. We know you'd be convinced. If we wasn't sure of that, we wouldn't show it to you."

"That sounds fair enough," said Blanton, "but it's not for me."

Cleve and Pat refused to take no for an answer. Cord kept the talk going until he was convinced it had accomplished its purpose. After regretfully declining the opportunity offered him for the twentieth time, he started to leave. His step slowed at the door, however, and he turned back to say, "You boys meet me across the street tomorrow morning at Robbins's place about nine o'clock. I'll pay for the assay. I'll go that far with you."

A cadaverous-looking Chinese, who had been hovering outside the swinging doors of the Silver Dollar all the while Cord was within, padded away, his gaunt face expressionless, as the latter stepped out. He had been an interested eavesdropper on the conversation between Blanton and his lieutenants, and not by accident. Judged by his cheap, ill-fitting garments, he might have been one of the score or more Chinese gardeners who tilled tiny patches down in the wash and supplied Wolf River with fresh vegetables in season. Such was not the case, however; Lum Duck was not only an experienced desert prospector in his own right but the shrewd and canny agent of a Chinese co-operative mining company of whose existence white men were completely unaware.

Blanton was so well satisfied with himself over the way his plans were moving that he paid Lum Duck no attention; Wolf River had a sizable Chinese quarter, and he had become accustomed to seeing Orientals shuffling along the street at all hours of the day and night.

But a thought flashed across his mind after he had taken a dozen steps that swung him around sharply. The Chinese had quickened his pace, and when he reached the path that led over the sagebrush-covered hill to Chinatown, he began to run, his face no longer an expressionless mask.

"I'd like to know the meaning of that!" Cord growled to himself. "That Chink got an earful and he's high-tailing it home with what he heard!"

An explanation suggested itself to him at once, and it swept away all his composure. Weeks ago, in Reno, he had warned Pat and Cleve to be on the lookout for Chinese prospectors. He knew the Chinese had penetrated many of the deepest recesses of that vast wasteland below Toquima Basin.

Some Chinks must have spotted them! Cord thought. *That's what is behind this!*

It didn't satisfy him. Perhaps Cleve and McGarry had allowed themselves to be drawn into a fight with them.

That would explain why the damned fools were four days late getting here! We'll be in a fine fix if we're going to have a gang of Chinamen keeping cases on us! I'll find out about this right now!

A flash of sense stopped him as he started to return to the Silver Dollar; he couldn't afford to have it out with Cleve and Pat in front of the others; he'd have to wait till he could get them alone.

"All right, I'll wait!" he muttered. "But I'll get to the bottom of this in the morning!"

Chapter Four

DIRTY WORK AT WOLF RIVER

CORD WAS DOWN EARLY for breakfast, after having spent a restless night. It didn't occur to him that it was his own nerves that were wearing thin and that the circumstances didn't warrant the tempests he was getting into. Heretofore, he had been able to keep himself on an even keel, no matter on what he was engaged. That certainly had not been the case of late.

He knew Perce Robbins never got down to his office before nine. He had told Cleve and Pat to be there at that hour. In the hope that they would be there ahead of time, he sailed out of the hotel a few minutes after eight and hurried up the street.

There was no one at Perce's door. A quarter of an hour and more passed before Miller and McGarry hove into sight. The waiting had enraged Cord, and he was set to let the two men feel it.

"Say, boss, we did all right last night, didn't we?" Cleve got out gleefully before Blanton could say a word. "We didn't miss a—"

"You did all right!" Cord cut him off sharply. "Suppose you shut up and let me do the talking. When I came out of the saloon last evening, I bumped into a Chinaman who'd been standing at the door, listening to what we said. Did you guys have a run-in with some of them fellas?"

It drew an emphatic no from both.

"After we got fifty miles out of Sodaville, we didn't see a soul," Pat told him.

"We had that country to ourselves," Cleve agreed.

Blanton regarded them with a cold eye.

"Is that on the level?"

"It sure is!" Cleve insisted. "We saw some tracks after we got north of Spanish Tanks. They was so old they was beginning to drift over. That was all."

"Then what in hell happened to you?" Cord rapped. "You was four days late getting here. I'd given you up."

"We ran into a sandstorm in the basin," Pat answered. "We had to turn around and drift south with it till we could find a place where we could hole up till it blew itself out. We was there a couple days before we could git goin' ag'in." Blanton's distrustful attitude had begun to get under McGarry's skin and he let him know it. "We was short of rations, too. We figgered we did purty well to come through at all. It don't seem to be appreciated. What's eatin' you, Cord?"

"Plenty! I don't want none of these yellow gents keeping cases on us. They got tongues; they talk, same as white men. I didn't know what had happened. If you think it was any picnic for me to sit here and see the days going by without word from you, you're crazy!"

"That don't sound like you—getting steamed up over nothing," Cleve remarked pointedly. "You're usually ice when the pinch is on. You want to get a grip on yourself."

"Forget it!" Cord snapped. "Now that I know what happened, it's okay. We won't say no more about it. Just watch your step; we're going to move fast."

"His nibs showed up yet?" Cleve asked.

"Greenwood?"

"Yeah."

Cord shook his head.

"He's due. There's mail waiting for him at the hotel. When this fellow Robbins shows up, don't let him stall you. You boys tell him you want this assay made this morning. This is him coming now. He's a gabby old fogy. Don't let him get to gassing with you."

Perce Robbins had conducted his assaying business in Wolf River for many years. The pickings had often been so poor that he had been forced to take on various side lines. He had never permitted adversity to get him down. An enormously tall man, well over sixty now and thin as a rail, he still had a springy step and a pair of clear-blue eyes that retained a sparkle of youth. Wolf River had never appreciated his competence until the big Midas Mountain Mining Company had turned all its assaying over to him.

"Good morning, gentlemen!" he greeted his callers cheerily. "The mayor just stopped me for a word as I came up the street. He told me I could expect you to drop in. According to Tom, there's no question that you've found something. I'm anxious to see what you've got."

He unlocked the door and invited them to step in.

The little storeroom was neatly arranged. One side was given over to a display of postcards and an assortment of novelties, most of which looked as though they had been on the shelves a long time. A shallow glass-topped showcase covered the counter. It contained a collection of gold-, silver-, and copper-bearing ore samples that he had gathered through the years, among them the specimens Johnnie Bidwell had brought in in the long ago.

"We're in something of a hurry," Cleve announced. "How soon can you give us the word on what we've got here?"

THE LOST BUCKAROO   43

"That depends on what oxides are present," Perce replied. "I have a little work to finish for the Midas Company. But I'd say I'll be ready for you tomorrow morning."

"You'll have to do better than that," said Cord. "I've agreed to pay for the assay. Whether I go any further depends on your report. I expect to go north tomorrow morning, so I'll have to know this afternoon."

"I'm sorry to hear you're leaving us, Mr. Blanton," Perce declared. "Not for good, I hope."

"That depends," said Cord. "What do you say?"

"I can make it this afternoon, if you insist. Let me see the samples."

He sat down at his desk and spilled out the contents of the small canvas bag Pat handed him. With smothered exclamations of mingled surprise and delight, he turned the fragments of rocks over and over with his long, sensitive fingers, treating them as though they were the most precious of jewels.

He selected one piece and examined it under his microscope.

"Remarkable!" he observed. "Remarkable!" He was as excited as a bird dog that had just picked up a fresh scent.

"What do you mean—remarkable?" Cleve demanded suspiciously. "You can see the values in that stuff with the naked eye!"

"Of course! Gold and some silver. That's not what surprises me. Gentlemen, I understand you made your find somewhere south of Toquima Basin—in the general region of the Monitors and the Solomons. Is that correct?"

"Yeah," Cleve answered again. "What's that got to do with it?"

Perce pushed back his chair and shook his head in an expression of bewilderment.

"Well, gentlemen, you see, I'm something of an amateur geologist as well as an assayer. In all the years I have examined specimens of syenite granite, with quartz as the chief base, found in that region, this is the first time I ever saw both black mica and feldspar crystals in it. The composition of the syenite granites varies remarkably in different parts of Nevada. Such a formation as this is the usual thing in the Tonopah-Goldfield district and across the line in California. I would have said it just didn't occur in this part of the state, and I'm sure such a well-known authority as Professor Greenwood, of the Mackay School of Mines, would agree with me."

It rang a warning bell in Cord Blanton's brain. He had thought of everything, only to slip up on this. Pat had acquired these samples in Tonopah.

"It just goes to show that most of this scientific stuff doesn't mean a thing when you really get down to it," Cord asserted. He knew something had to be said in a hurry, and he dared not leave it to either Cleve or McGarry, who were frankly dumfounded. "It's like doctoring; they go along with a theory until someone turns up something new that proves them wrong, then they start guessing all over again. I'm no expert, but I guess Nevada's got a few secrets that no one knows anything about yet."

Robbins wagged his head in agreement.

"I'll say amen to that! We've barely scratched the surface. This is a case in point. If you'll drop in around four o'clock, I'll be ready for you."

Cord got Cleve and Pat outside and walked toward the hotel with them.

"That was a close call!" he growled. "That old duffer spotted the stuff for what it is."

"You think he's suspicious?" McGarry asked.

"No," Cord replied. "I figured if I said too much he might smell a rat. Where did you get that ore, Pat?"

"The Tonopah Consolidated. It's seventy-dollar ore. I didn't want to git anythin' too rich." McGarry heaved a sigh of relief. "I thought he had us there, fer a minute. What do we do now?"

"You and Cleve stay away from me; I don't want to appear to be getting too friendly with you. Meet me at the hotel a few minutes before four, and we'll go down together. Robbins won't hold back on what he finds. By the time we hear the good news it'll be all over town. The two of you will persuade me to come in with you. We'll get our outfit together this evening and pull out in the morning."

His prediction that Perce Robbins wouldn't keep his findings a secret proved to be an understatement. Seventy-dollar ore, if there was enough of it, was something to get excited about. One man told another, and by four o'clock it was the chief topic of conversation in Wolf River.

When Cord walked into the office with Pat and Miller, they found Tom Stewart and several of the town's merchants there, all eager to congratulate them on their luck.

Cord read the report and handed it over to Pat and Cleve. The latter pretended to be disappointed.

"I'd figured it'd run higher than that," he declared. It was acting of a rather high order. "The silver doesn't amount to anything, eh?"

"It doesn't run high enough to be worth anything commercially," said Perce. "You needn't worry about that; when you've got cake, you don't have to eat bread." He chuckled over his own jest. "If you've got ore like this in quantity, and it's get-at-able, so it won't cost you too much to get it out, you've got a rich proposition on your hands, my boys."

"That's the question." Blanton spoke up. "How much is there, and how much is it going to cost to get it to mill? It'll be a long haul."

"We got the ore," Cleve assured him. "We'll show you plenty. Ain't that right, Pat?"

"Sure," the latter agreed. "We can work right along the fault. Not a foot of road will have to be built."

"Sounds good to me, Blanton," Stewart volunteered. "I don't want to crowd you out; you got first call. But if you ain't interested, I'll buy a piece of it."

This made it even easier for Cord.

"I didn't say I wasn't interested," he remarked. He turned to Cleve. "If I staked you, how soon could we be ready to pull out?"

"I don't know. Most any time. Won't take us long to throw together what we need. We can make it tomorrow morning if you say so."

Cord hesitated, and not because he didn't have his answer ready. A Chinese, who had evidently been in the back room, moved in with broom and dustpan and went about his work with what appeared to be a complete lack of interest in what was being said in the front of the store.

Cord watched him suspiciously and caught him listening.

"Mr. Robbins, does your Chinaman usually come in at this hour of the day to clean up your place?"

Perce straightened up, surprised at the hostility in Blanton's voice.

"Chin comes in whenever he gets a chance. He's got a number of places along the street that he looks after. Anything wrong with him, Mr. Blanton?"

"He's got long ears," Cord said thinly. "I don't like it! If it's just the same to you, tell him to get out of here till we've finished our business."

"As you please," Perce agreed indulgently. "Chin is perfectly harmless, but I'll tell him to come back and finish up tomorrow."

He spoke to the man. The Chinese put away the tools of his trade and shuffled out.

"What made you blow up like that, Blanton?" Stewart asked. "We think a lot of that old boy around town."

"I suppose you do. I've got nothing against him." Cord's tone was apologetic. "But I don't like the idea of having the business I'm discussing with McGarry and Miller spread all over Chinatown. Lots of these Chinks are out looking for gold. They're all over the desert. I'm considering putting money into unregistered claims. Be a hell of a note if some of those highbinders got a line on things and jumped them."

Tom and the Wolf River men had a hearty laugh at his expense, with the mayor ridiculing the idea that Cord would have any trouble with old Chin or his countrymen.

"You're gittin' spooked up over nothin'," Tom declared. "In my forty years around this part of Nevada, I never heard of a Chinaman jumpin' another man's claim. I *can* tell you of a number of occasions when they went into the desert for white men that was lost and brought 'em out alive. Don't git the Chinese down on you, Blanton; you may need them."

Cord waved the advice aside.

"Don't get me wrong, Tom; I ain't looking for trouble. I just aim to make sure I don't run into any."

He paid Perce his fee for the assay. He turned to Pat and Cleve then.

"I'm going to gamble with you fellas. Come up to the hotel and make out a list of what you need and I'll give you the money. If this thing is a dud, the sooner I find out the better."

They got away shortly after daybreak the next morning. In the late afternoon, Henry Greenwood and the giant Moy Kim arrived on the mixed train from the north. They brought with them their desert outfit, including the two dependable burros they had used for several years.

The professor was well known in Wolf River. After registering at the Union House, the first old friend he called on was Perce Robbins. Perce had startling news for him. Greenwood's face fell as he listened.

"I hadn't expected to be met with anything like this, Perce. Do you mean to say it's the Lost Buckaroo they've found?"

"No! No! Not at all, Henry! It's an entirely different formation. I held out a piece of their ore to show you. My eyes popped when I saw their samples. It's going to give you one of the biggest surprises of your life. Syenite, with crystallized black mica and feldspar running all through it!"

"In central Nevada? I can't believe it!" The professor's tone was frankly incredulous.

Robbins chuckled.

"I said you'd be surprised. Here, take a look at it."

A startled exclamation escaped Greenwood as he examined the jagged fragment of rock.

"You're right, Perce!" he acknowledged. "Let me sit down and put it under the lens."

He studied the sample long and carefully.

"Well, what do you make of it, Henry?"

"I don't know," was the honest answer. "I'm dumfounded. It certainly isn't the Lost Buckaroo. But that's beside the point; this is something that runs contrary to every established fact. I'd give most anything I own just to have a look at this vein. Do you know anything about the two men who found it?"

Robbins gave him what information he possessed.

"I know there's always the possibility of a freak formation showing up," he continued. "But there could be another explanation, Henry. It wouldn't be the first time the game has been worked. We've only got their word for it that the samples they brought in came from below the basin. They admitted they were down on their luck. They could have faked up their story to get themselves a new grubstake. Their samples may have come from anywhere. This man Blanton thinks he's a shrewd customer. But he's a saloonkeeper, he doesn't know too much about mining. Miller and McGarry could be playing him for a sucker."

Greenwood smiled skeptically.

"That's an interesting speculation, Perce, but it doesn't hold water. They know they'll have to show him something or he'll walk out on them. Maybe I'll run into them down there. I hope so. I'd certainly like to examine their property."

It was his intention to leave Wolf River not later than noon of the following day and spend the night at the Jensen ranch on Calamity Creek. He talked freely of his plans, as was his way, and he didn't forget to ask about one of his old students, who had graduated from the School of Mines several years back.

"I don't know what's become of William Chew," Robbins told him. "He had a good job as one of the assistant engineers with the Midas Company, but he gave that up months ago. He used to drop in here and chat with me every few days. His old man is still the kingpin of Chinatown. I asked Quan about the boy some time ago. He was evasive. Chinamen don't tell you anything when they don't want to. I suppose Willie is out prospecting. He might be looking for the Lost Buckaroo, Henry."

"He might at that—and be smart enough to find it."

Greenwood dismissed it without a second thought. William Chew, a Nevada-born Chinese, had always been one of his favorites. The boy had a good mind and had easily earned his degree, the first of his race to do so.

"If you see his father, tell him I was asking about William. I'm going to get out of here now; Moy and I have plenty to do if we're going to get away tomorrow."

They had everything put together by midmorning and were on their way by noon. Before long, they found themselves following the tracks Blanton and his companions had left.

"Following in their footsteps," Greenwood mused. "Too bad I was a day late; we could have gone in together."

He was all unsuspicious, and when he turned for a farewell glance at the town, he said, "Better take a last look at it, Kim. It will be a long time before we see it again."

Moy nodded solemnly.

"Be long time, missa boss."

It was to be much longer than either suspected, for they were never to see Wolf River again.

Chapter Five

JIM McBRIDE, chief of Wells Fargo detectives in the Denver district, sat at his desk this September morning, a broad grin of satisfaction erasing the lines that the past eighteen months had engraved in his face. He was a former Pinkerton man, as were many of the men who served under him.

His secretary broke in on his altogether pleased contemplation of the good news he had received.

"Mr. Ripley and Mr. Gibbs are here," she informed him.

"Send them in, Miss Crozier. I've been waiting for them."

He swung around in his swivel chair and greeted the partners as they appeared in the doorway.

"You were lucky to catch us, Jim," Rainbow informed him. "We were just about to pull out for Pueblo when we got your message. What's up?"

"Well, boys, the long hunt's over. I had a wire from Sharpless about an hour ago. I'll read it to you. 'We took Snedeker and the Johnsons into custody last night after gun fight ten miles east of town Stop Just brought them in Stop Lonnie Johnson ready to sing.' "

"That does it, I reckon!" Grumpy remarked, with his characteristic crustiness.

McBride nodded.

"It's the old story, boys. Wells Fargo never forgets. That's as true today as when Dan O'Brien first said it, years ago. We needed some outside help this time, and it proved to be considerable. We can thank the two of you that we've wound this thing up at last. Been eighteen months since those birds looted that express car at La Junta."

"If you're satisfied, we are," said Rainbow. "Naturally, Grump and I would have preferred to snag those fellows ourselves."

They had come into the case long after all the clues were cold and the most plausible leads had been run down without producing any results. When Grumpy and he had first suggested that Red Snedeker and the Johnson brothers were the men they wanted, the idea had been ridiculed. Rip mentioned the fact now.

"I admit it," McBride declared. "You made us eat crow. You going to stick around Denver a few days?"

"No, we're anxious to get back to Wyoming. We haven't been home in over three months. You can mail our check to us at Black Forks."

The partners found themselves on the street a few minutes later.

"I'm glad we're done with that job," the little one grumbled. "Good pay, and that's all I can say for it."

"That's saying considerable for it," Rainbow countered laughingly. He knew it was the endless conferences and the routine of the Wells Fargo case that were responsible for Grumpy's complaint. "I might as well admit I wasn't too happy, either. Fact is, we've been on our own so long that we're not gaited to work with other men. Anyhow, we'll be getting home at a good time; September is always the pleasantest month of the year on the ranch. It'll be good to see the Judge and the boys again."

"It shore will!" was the hearty response. "We ain't seen much of Bar 7 since spring."

They spoke about the range they had been putting together and stocking for several years. Thanks to the kindness of their long-time friend, Judge Benton Carver, his Bar 7 crew worked it for the partners and refused to accept any reimbursement.

"We've often talked about buildin' a house on the place," Grumpy remarked. "Was **that** jest talk, or are we goin' to do it?"

"I don't know," said Rainbow. "I haven't given it much thought. You don't sound enthusiastic about it."

"Wal, I dunno as I am," the little man declared. "Bar 7 is home to me, and I don't want no better. A man builds a house, and the next thing he does is take a wife."

"That seems to be the way it goes," Rip agreed. "Have you any intentions in that direction?" he inquired innocently.

Grumpy dismissed the question with a snort of disgust.

"That nonsense is for kids and old fools, and I ain't neither!"

"Oh, I don't know," Rip pursued, keeping a straight face. "They say a man never really knows what life means till he marries."

"Yeah, and then it's too late. Suppose you stop tryin' to needle me; I'm more interested in eatin' some lunch."

"Okay," said Rip. "We'll walk up to the Brown. Something may have come in for us."

When they checked out of the hotel that morning they had expected to be gone only a day or two and had left word to have their mail held.

Their bags were already at the Union Depot. Aside from reserving Pullman space on the evening train to Cheyenne, they had the rest of the day to themselves. It wasn't often they found themselves with so much time on their hands. To spend it in Denver promised to be a pleasant chore.

A bellhop came running after them as they crossed the lobby of the Brown and informed Rainbow that he was wanted at the desk.

The clerk was waiting for him with a letter.

"I just saw you going into the café, Mr. Ripley," the clerk explained. "This letter came in on the eleven o'clock delivery. It's marked 'Rush' and 'Important.' "

Rip thanked him. The letter had been forwarded from Black Forks. He recognized Judge Carver's scholarly handwriting. Of even greater interest to him was the return address on the envelope.

"What is it?" Grumpy inquired, as they waited for a table.

"It'll surprise you. It's from Wolf River, Nevada."

"From our friend Greenwood?"

"No. I imagine the professor has been back in Reno for some time. This is from the office of the president of the Midas Mountain Mining Company."

After ordering lunch, Rainbow opened the letter. The letterhead, embossed with a picture of Midas Mountain, showing the company's stamp mills and smelter, was impressive.

"This is a substantial outfit," the tall man observed. When he had finished reading, he smiled across the table at Grumpy. "Brother, if you're still interested in seeing Wolf River, here's your chance. This C. B. Macgruder, the president of the company, says they have evidence that they're being high-graded. The sheriff has not been able to get to the bottom of it, and he wants us to take over. Seems the district attorney out there, Dennis Mc-Caffery, has recommended us to him."

Rip passed the letter over to his partner. The little man put on his gold-rimmed spectacles and digested its contents. When he looked up from it there was a puzzled light in his eyes.

"Somethin' about this I don't git," he said. "If yo're takin' out rich ore and you know somebody's makin' off with some of it, it ain't usually no trick to find out who's takin' it. I reckon there's more to it than what this letter says."

"Undoubtedly," Rainbow agreed. "He asks us to get in touch with him at once. What do you want to do about it?"

"Tell him we'll be out there next week. No reason why we should pass up a job; we can stop off in Black Forks for the week-end."

"We better forget about Black Forks," Rip advised. "This letter is five days old right now."

"Okay!" Grumpy grumbled. "Wire Macgruder we're on the way. Wednesday, Thursday—we ought to be there on Friday," he added, counting the days with his fingers.

"Late Friday. I'm going to tell Mr. Macgruder to meet us in the district attorney's office. It would be a mistake to go near the mine until we know what the facts are. We used to be able to slip into one of these Nevada towns and be there two or three days before our business became known. We can't do that any more, we've been out there too often. Chances are we won't be in Wolf River an hour before somebody spots us."

Rainbow's surmise was borne out almost as soon as they stepped down from the train in Wolf River. Cleve Miller chanced to be at the depot. He recognized them at once. The depot was the equivalent of two city blocks from the main street. Keeping them in sight, he saw them go directly to the courthouse, without even stopping to leave their bags at the hotel. Fearful of what it meant, he lost no time getting to the Silver Dollar.

The saloon had changed hands recently. Russian Louie was gone, and Cord Blanton was the new proprietor. The place had undergone a minor face lifting, but it had not been transformed into the ornate establishment Blanton had promised Wolf River. He still talked about it. It was only talk, however; the Silver Dollar was just an excuse for his continued presence in town.

Cleve found Cord in his office at the rear of the saloon. He broke in on him with unconcealed excitement.

"This will give you something to think about!" he whipped out. "Rainbow Ripley and his sidekick just hit town. They went straight to the courthouse."

Cord started to dismiss the news contemptuously, only to change his mind.

"You sure?" he demanded thinly.

"You bet I'm sure! What the hell is that pair doing here if it ain't got something to do with Greenwood? He was their friend. We been kidding ourselves, Cord; we ain't out of the woods yet!"

Blanton's face was suddenly tight and hard.

"Is Pat outside?"

"Yeah—"

"Get him in here!" Cord commanded.

When McGarry was informed of the situation, he became as alarmed as Miller.

"I don't care what brought 'em to Wolf River; they're goin' to hear things and start askin' questions. I'm tellin' you, Cord, when that pair gits their noses to the ground, they're poison!"

"You guys better get over your panic!" Blanton

warned. "If you got any brains, you want to use 'em! Our story was okay; nobody questioned it. We'll be all right if we stick to it. Don't you fools try to change a word of it! If those dicks get around to asking you questions, don't walk away from them. That would be the worst thing you could do. Be friendly—helpful—and be damned careful what you say!"

He didn't let them go until he was convinced that they understood to the letter what their role was to be.

"You can keep an eye on them, but don't let them get the idea you're watching them. If anything has to be done, I'll tell you what, and when."

Barely more than a stone's throw away, Rip and Grumpy had just learned that Henry Greenwood and Moy Kim had not been heard from since they disappeared into the desert, three months ago.

Seated with them in the district attorney's office were McCaffery and Shep Logan, the sheriff. Word had been sent to Macgruder, and he was expected down from the mine momentarily.

The news about Greenwood shocked the partners.

"I suppose some effort was made to find him?" said Rainbow.

"I went out three times," Logan replied. "Others went out, too. Perce Robbins, a good friend of Greenwood, organized a group of men that went way down into the Solomons. They didn't find any trace of him. Greenwood and his Chinaman are dead and have been for weeks. No question about that."

"You figger they got lost or ran out of water?" Grumpy asked.

Logan shook his head.

"Mac and I are convinced they got caught in a cloudburst and were drowned. You never saw so much water as we had back in July. One cloudburst after another. There was over ten feet of water in the wash at one time. It tore out everything and came within a foot or two of wiping out Chinatown. They got it even worse below here. I got pretty far down into the Monitors and the Solomons. That country's all torn up. I saw half a dozen places where a torrent had poured down a canyon. No vegetation to hold the sand. You can imagine what it was like."

"It's hard to believe that an experienced desert man like Henry Greenwood could have been trapped that way," said Rainbow. "What about their burros and camp gear?"

"Not a sign of anything. You know, Ripley, when a cloudburst hits you, it comes all at once. If you're caught in a canyon and can't get to high ground in a hurry, it's apt to be just too bad."

"There's a saloonkeeper in town, by the name of Blanton, who was down in that country the same time Greenwood was," McCaffery said in corroboration. "He had two men with him. They had a close shave. Lost their burros and everything. They managed to stagger into a ranch on Calamity Creek. They'd been without grub and water for four or five days. The only way to get them to town was to put them in a wagon and drive them in."

"They didn't see anythin' of Greenwood?"

"They say they didn't see anyone. There's always Wolf River Chinamen prospecting in the Monitors. I questioned Quan Chew, the boss of Chinatown, hoping he could give us some information. He says his men are all accounted for and that they didn't see any white men."

"It's too bad," Grumpy declared soberly. "The professor was so shore he was goin' to find the Lost Buckaroo this summer. We spent an evenin' with him in Reno, back in June. His daughter must be takin' it awful hard. They seemed to be mighty close to each other."

McCaffery nodded grimly.

"That's the tough part about it. It hasn't been easy to face her. She's been here to see Shep and me three or four times. At first, we held out some hope to her, though we knew there wasn't any. We finally had to tell her the truth. We had a time doing it. She isn't completely convinced even now her father's gone; she insists that if he is he was murdered."

The statement had an electrifying effect on the partners.

"Let me get this straight," said Rainbow. "Is it Miss Greenwood's contention that her father found the Lost Buckaroo and was killed defending it?"

"I'd say that's exactly what she thinks," McCaffery replied. "She has nothing to justify such a contention, but she's taken that stand and won't be talked out of it."

"She must have some reason for thinkin' what she does," Grumpy spoke up. "We found her a mighty sensible young woman."

"I'll second that," said Rip. "It isn't likely she's knowingly holding back on any knowledge she might have. Just what does she say?"

"Oh, that everyone knew her father was after the Lost Buckaroo and he had told so many people he'd surely find it this summer that someone may have been lying in wait for him. Also, that Wolf River is just one way of getting into Toquima Basin and the mountains to the south, that we can never say who is in that country, or how many men are there. Now that's all very true, but there isn't a shred of evidence in it that Henry Greenwood and his Chink met with foul play."

"Is that all she has to go on?" Rainbow pursued.

"No, she has a letter from her father, mailed from Wolf River. Greenwood had been out about three weeks, when he sent his man into town for fresh supplies. He brought the letter in and mailed it. I've read it. Greenwood doesn't give any locations, but he says he's found certain formations and strata that will positively lead him to the mine in a few days."

Dennis McCaffery, able young lawyer that he was, expressed what he felt about it with a doubting smile.

"Henry Greenwood was inclined to be overly optimistic," he observed pointedly. "Maybe he wasn't looking for something that never was; I wouldn't know about that. But there's no evidence that he found the Lost Buckaroo or some other rich deposit—call it what you will—and certainly there isn't the slightest reason to believe he lost his life protecting something he had found."

He got up and walked to the window.

"Macgruder ought to be showing up," he said. "There he is now, coming up the street."

Rip and Grumpy were silent. The disappearance of Henry Greenwood had become of greater interest to them than the problems of the Midas Mountain Mining Company.

"There's one thing Mac didn't mention," Logan, the sheriff, volunteered. "You might as well hear it all. When Greenwood's Chink came back for supplies, he bought two rifles and a quantity of cartridges. His daughter says her father never went armed and the fact that he wanted rifles is proof enough that he considered himself in danger."

"Wal, that makes sense to me!" Grumpy exclaimed.

"There ain't no game in that country, is there?"

"Not a bit," Logan answered.

"Then how do you gentlemen explain his sudden need of guns?" Rainbow inquired. "Surely he could have felt he needed them for only one reason."

"I think the logical explanation is that Greenwood honestly believed he was about to put his hands on the Lost Buckaroo," declared McCaffery, "which would have meant leaving the Chinaman at the mine while he came into town to file his papers and get legal title to the property. I presume he felt that arming the man with a rifle would be using just ordinary precaution."

It failed to satisfy Rainbow.

"It'll take more explanation than that—considerably more," said he. "Moy Kim would not have needed two rifles. Before we leave Nevada, we'll go to Reno and have a talk with Miss Greenwood."

McCaffery took it as an affront to the sheriff and himself, reading into it an implied criticism of their efforts.

"I don't believe it'll be necessary for you to leave Wolf River to do that," he said stiffly. "I had a letter from her several weeks ago, telling me she had sold her home and that she was coming here to stay until she found her father, dead or alive. I hope the two of you will be of some assistance to her."

Rip caught the thinly veiled sarcasm in the young district attorney's tone.

"I didn't mean to step on your toes," he hastened to say. "You and Logan have done everything you could. We may not be able to get any farther than you have. On the other hand, Henry Greenwood was an old friend of ours; we're indebted to him for numerous favors. It seems the least we can do is to offer our services to his daughter."

Chapter Six

HARD-BOILED CUSTOMER

CHARLIE MACGRUDER, the president and principal stockholder of the multimillion-dollar Midas Mountain Mining Company, was a baldish little man with a jerky, nervous manner of speaking. What he had to say to Rip and Grumpy was so far from what they expected that they didn't attempt to conceal their amazement.

"We gathered from your letter that the high-grading was an established fact and had attained sizable proportions," Rip told him. "That doesn't appear to be the case at all. As near as I can gather, you are more concerned about what may be happening than what you can point to as a definite fact."

"That's true," Macgruder agreed. "There's a leak somewhere; we know that. The few ounces of gold we can trace can hardly be the extent of the thieving that's going on."

"Has the cat been let out of the bag?" Grumpy asked. "Who knows about it as of now?"

"McCaffery, Shep, Tom Williams, my superintendent, and myself."

Rainbow turned to Logan.

"Sheriff, have you questioned anyone?"

"No," was the prompt answer.

"Nothing has been said to this Chinese, Lum Duck, who sold the gold to the mint at Carson?"

"I purposely kept away from him," said Logan. "Mac

and I talked it over. We figured we couldn't question him without making him suspicious. It seemed a lot more sensible to let the game go on till we found out how it was being worked and who was involved."

"I certainly agree with that," said Rip. "Let's see just what we've got in the way of facts. Lum Duck buys gold ore, presumably most of his business is with Chinese prospectors. About once a month he sells his ore—at least part of it—to the branch U. S. mint at Carson City. Your company, Mr. Macgruder, disposes of all its gold to the mint. Recently, and for the third time, the Government metallurgists have notified you that part of the ore they have bought from Lum Duck is from your mine."

"They have ways of proving such things, Mr. Ripley," Macgruder broke in. "It's not open to question."

"I'm not questioning it at all," Rainbow informed him. "I agree that it's entirely plausible, too, that the mint may be getting only a fraction of the gold Lum Duck sells. I presume he has a store in Chinatown."

"He has a small shop in which he conducts his business," McCaffery answered. "Shep has had the place under surveillance for some time. Lum Duck does no business with white men, and only white men are employed in the mine."

"Do yore men live on company property or in town, Mr. Macgruder?" Grumpy questioned.

"Here in town. We have a commissary where they eat dinner. When they arrive in the morning, they get into their work clothes and get out of them again when they go off shift. We watch them pretty carefully."

"Yore foreman and supers above suspicion?"

"Absolutely! We've taken every possible safeguard. I tell you, gentlemen, it just about passes belief that even an ounce of gold is being stolen. And yet we know it's happening."

The conference dragged on for some time, without producing anything of importance.

"We seem to have gone as far as we can for now," Rip said at last. "We'll come up to the mine in the morning and look things over. It may take some time to run this down. Unfortunately, my partner and I can't keep our presence in Wolf River a secret. There'll be some speculation as to why we're here; but let me urge you to go on as you have in the past, saying nothing to any one."

The meeting broke up a few minutes later, and the partners walked up the street to the Union House. From their connecting rooms on the second floor they had a good view of the town and Midas Mountain, with its mills and smelter. As for Wolf River, it was as like other Nevada towns they had known as peas in a pod.

Grumpy pulled off his boots and got out his pipe, bent on relaxing before supper. His grizzled face wore a thoughtful frown.

"This young McCaffery is a mite touchy," he observed. "He'll have to be handled with kid gloves. We'll get along all right with Logan."

"We should," Rainbow answered from the washstand, where he was shaving.

Grumpy smoked in silence for several minutes.

"What do you think we've run into, Rip?" he asked without warning.

"The Midas job, you mean?"

"No, Greenwood. This talk of him bein' caught by a cloudburst and drowned don't sound right to me."

The tall man cleaned his razor carefully. Over his shoulder, he said soberly, "I suspect he was murdered. But we better reserve judgment on that till we can sit down with Lane Greenwood and hear what she has to say. About this high-grading, I don't know what to think, beyond the fact that the two things don't tie together."

"What makes you so shore about that?" the little one queried skeptically.

"Grump, if Greenwood was murdered it was only because he'd found the Lost Buckaroo. With a stake like that in their hands, the men who killed him wouldn't be interested in high-grading."

It silenced the little man.

"McCaffery mentioned that a saloonkeeper by the name of Blanton was down in that country and got caught. After supper we'll drop into his place and let him talk, if he will."

The suggestion met with Grumpy's approval, and after a leisurely supper they learned from the hotel clerk where Cord could be found.

The Silver Dollar was crowded, for a Friday night, when the partners strolled in. Blanton had already made the place more popular than when Russian Louie owned it. In line with the custom he had followed in Tonopah, he never appeared behind his own bar. He believed it gave the place a certain air of distinction for him to circulate among his customers, and it also gave him an opportunity to keep a watchful eye on his bartenders.

He was on the floor when Rip and Grumpy came in. Cleve Miller gave him the word at once. Cord was prepared for it. He waited until the partners had their drinks served before he nonchalantly strolled toward them, his interest apparently impersonal. He saw Rip speak to the bartender. The latter jerked his head in Cord's direction.

It was an invitation for Blanton to step up.

"Gentlemen, what can I do for you?" he asked, professionally affable.

Rip introduced himself and Grumpy.

"This is an honor," said Cord. "I've often heard of you. I thought I hadn't seen you in Wolf River before."

"We jest got in this afternoon," Grumpy informed him. "Young McCaffery, the district attorney, tells us you was down in the desert the same time Henry Greenwood was. He was an old friend of ours."

"I didn't know him," said Cord. "No one can say exactly what happened to him, but I suppose he got caught the same way we did. Let's find a table; we can sit down. I'll have your drinks sent over."

Though he wanted to give the impression that he was speaking freely and had nothing to hold back, he weighed every word carefully as he related how Miller, McGarry, and he had come within an inch of losing their lives.

"Get me away from town and I'm a rank tenderfoot," he said. "Miller talks a lot about what he knows, but most of it's just wind. Pat was the one we had to depend on; he got us out."

"How did you git hooked up with 'em?" Grumpy asked.

Cord considered he was on safe ground now, and he told the story as Wolf River knew it. He had repeated it so often that it had acquired a ring of truth. Rip and Grumpy found no reason to question it.

"The way things turned out, yo're sorta left holdin' the bag," the little one remarked.

"Yes," Cord acknowledged, with a wry smile, "but I can't blame the boys for that; when we lost our outfit, there was nothing we could do but turn back and try to get out alive. All the gold I've seen so far was in the samples they brought in. But we'll have another try at it this fall, when it's too late for the weather to act up."

"Are Miller and McGarry still around town?" asked Rainbow.

"Yeah, I'm staking them. I get some work out of them; Miller fills in behind the bar on Saturday nights. I don't see Pat just now, but Miller's here. I'll call him over if you want to talk to him."

"Don't bother," said Rip. "We'll be dropping in again. We've got some business here."

Blanton did not make the mistake of expressing any curiosity regarding the nature of that business. He surmised what it was. But that wasn't good enough; he had to know for certain. Though he realized that he had learned exactly nothing this evening, he comforted himself with the thought that he had played a safe hand. There'd be other ways of getting the information he wanted.

"Drop in any time," he urged, as the partners were leaving. "If I ain't around, ask one of the boys."

Grumpy waited for Rainbow to express his opinion of Blanton. The tall man was strangely silent as they walked along.

"He got you puzzled?" the little one demanded finally.

"Slightly. I couldn't figure anything wrong with what he had to say. We can check on that. I gave him a chance to ask us what we're doing in Wolf River. I thought he might be interested."

"Mebbe he knows why we're here," Grumpy observed pointedly. "He's a shrewd, hard-boiled customer. I couldn't git the idea outa my mind as we was sittin' there that his joint might be the drop for the ore the Midas Company is losin'. Blanton must have some Chink doin' his porter work. It would be easy for him to pass the stuff along to this Lum Duck character."

"That's all right as a hunch," Rip objected, "but it could be true of any saloon in town. We'll do better if we tackle this thing at the source. Once we know how the ore is being smuggled off company property, the rest shouldn't be too difficult."

They spent the following day on the mountain, familiarizing themselves with the routine of the miners and workmen in the smelter. The work was handled in two shifts, the day shift coming on at seven in the morning and the night shift at the same hour in the evening. As Macgruder had stated, the men disrobed in a building used solely for that purpose, on their arrival, and repeated the dressing and undressing in reverse when they were through. Dinner buckets were not permitted; everyone ate in the commissary. Packages could not be taken out until they were inspected.

"You can see the extreme care we use," Macgruder remarked, as he sat at dinner in the commissary with the partners. "The ore we're taking out is so rich that we have to plug up every possible leak. And yet we're being gouged."

"You have spies in the dressing-room, I presume," said Rainbow.

"We have," was the frank admission. "We don't like it, but what else can we do?"

Rip let it pass without comment. The Chinese waiter placed their dessert on the table. The food was excellent and the place scrupulously clean, save for the muck the men tracked in on their boots. From the wizened little Chinese manager down to the dishwashers, the entire staff was Chinese.

Rainbow was wearing the jade ring Mei-lang had

placed on his finger one night in Black Rock, several years back. "The ring of the family of Seng," she had called it. Many times it had served him well in dealing with men of her race. Usually, when he found himself where Chinese were present and he preferred not to attract their attention, he turned the ring under. He had not done so today.

The waiter caught a glimpse of it, and his Oriental impassiveness was not equal to his surprise. Macgruder failed to notice, but Grumpy caught it, and he mentioned it to Rip as soon as they were alone.

"You usually turn it under. Did you forget?"

"No, it was deliberate, Grump. We've got to find some friends somewhere. Maybe those Chinese boys can help us to unravel this mystery."

A week slipped away on them. It became the usual thing for them to appear at the mine at any hour of the day or night. They weren't making any progress. Dropping in on the sheriff and McCaffery meant only further rehashing of what they knew before they first set foot on Midas Mountain.

The commissary had become their favorite rendezvous at the mine; no matter when they came in, there were always coffee and sandwiches awaiting them. Wu Ting, the manager, was always delighted to see them.

The partners came in one afternoon, about one-thirty, for coffee and pie. The men had gone back to work, and the commissary was deserted, save for two Chinese who were sweeping the floor. In back, the kitchen was noisy with the clatter of dishes. As they sat conversing with Ting, the sun glinted brightly on a fleck of gold on the floor. When one of the sweepers moved near it, Rip said, "Gold, there. See it?"

The Chinese showed his bad teeth in a vacant grin. He bent down, picked up the particle, and offered it to Rainbow.

"You wantee?"

Rip said no. He noticed that the man dropped the fleck of gold in his dustpan. The incident amused Wu Ting, or so he pretended.

"Mr. Ripley, you'd be surprised how much muck is tracked in every shift," he said. He spoke without a trace of pidgin. "It is wet in the mine. Wet boots pick up dust between here and the mine head, and we get it all."

"I've noticed," Rip told him. "It's remarkable how clean you keep the floor."

He said nothing to Grumpy at the time, but he began to observe how carefully the floor was always swept. Two nights later, he surprised the little man by telling him he had the answer to the riddle. Grumpy listened incredulously until he could stand no more.

"That's the craziest rot I ever heard from you!" he jeered. "It wouldn't amount to nothin'!"

"You can call it crazy if you want to," said Rip, "but I'm sticking with it. The ore Macgruder is taking out is so rich I hesitate to put a figure on it. I'd only be guessing if I did. I know even a little of it would be valuable. We've got the run of the commissary. What we've got to do is bust into the kitchen when we're least expected. If I'm right, we'll catch them, sooner or later."

They were in the commissary after dinner the following day and watched the sweeping. Fully a bushel of muck and dust went into a trash can and was carried to the kitchen. Soon after the work was finished, they stepped out. Twenty minutes later, they popped into the kitchen through a rear entrance. The evidence they sought was there before their eyes. At the sink, a Chinese was carefully washing the sweepings in a gold pan. The man tried to hide the pan, but it was too late. The ensuing excitement brought Wu Ting hurrying in. He realized what had happened.

"I do not appreciate your manner of discovering our secret," he said, holding himself in check, "but there is nothing wrong about what we are doing. This is my property; the land was deeded to me. I put up the building. We are not stealing the gold we extract from the sweepings. It is tracked into my place and would be thrown away but for my—"

"Just a minute, Ting," Rip interjected. "We don't know what the consequences of this will be. Perhaps you are legally entitled to the gold you recover. I hope so. But, however it goes, we want to befriend you, and we will if you give us a chance. I promise it on the ring of the family of Seng."

Ting regarded him keenly for a moment.

"What do you want me to do?"

"I want you to tell me the truth. From what I see in the pan, you must wash out almost an ounce a day. Am I right?"

"Some days. Not quite an ounce but nearly."

"And the same from the night shift?"

"It runs a little higher at night. I don't know why."

"Two ounces a day," Grumpy muttered. "That builds up. A thousand dollars a month, or so!"

"Ting—you sell your gold to Lum Duck. He sells it to the mint in Carson. It's been traced. So it's no secret. I want you to tell us, to the best of your knowledge, does he sell all of it in Carson, or is some being sold in California?"

"Mr. Ripley, there's so little—fifty to sixty ounces a month—why should he bother to find a customer, when the mint will take it all?"

The kitchen crew stood around, faces blank, understanding only part of what was being said.

"There's just one thing more," Rainbow told him. "You've kept an account of how much gold you've sold Lum Duck. What is the total, Ting?"

Wu Ting produced a small memorandum book, and after consulting it said, "Two hundred and four ounces. Mr. Macgruder must be made to understand we were not stealing the gold—"

"We won't say anything to him for the present. When we do, I believe we can reach an understanding that'll be satisfactory to both of you."

All that remained to do now was to question Lum Duck.

Driving down the mountain, Grumpy was painfully silent.

"What's the matter?" Rip inquired.

"Wal, I don't like to pull in my horns, but I reckon I'll have to this time. You was dead right all the way. What a joke this high-gradin' job has turned out to be! Bein' robbed blind, Macgruder thinks! He better keep his mouth shut and swallow this piddlin' loss, or he'll be laughed outa the country!"

They found Lum Duck in his shop. He didn't want to talk at first, but they persuaded him to change his mind. Before they were through with him they were convinced that the only Midas gold he had bought was what he got from Wu Ting.

"We can wind this thing up this afternoon," said Rip. "I'll fetch Macgruder down to the D.A.'s office. You see

McCaffery and Logan. Tell them we'll be there in an hour."

When they were gathered together in the district attorney's office later that afternoon, Rainbow dropped his bombshell. The sheriff and McCaffery saw the humor in the situation. Macgruder found it anything but amusing.

"Do you mean to say that's the extent of it?" he sputtered. "Why, I've been losing sleep and getting indigestion over this business!"

"You've been making a nervous wreck of yourself for nothing," Rip assured him. "Two hundred and four ounces in five months. I guess your company will survive. A white man would have swept that stuff out the door; only a Chinese would have had the patience to wash it out. If you want to stop it, you better have your men wash their boots."

"They'd take half an hour doing it, and it would cost us more than it's worth!" Macgruder snapped. "Besides, the men wouldn't stand for it! The gold Wu Ting sold didn't belong to him; he'll have to make good."

"I don't know whether you have any claim on it or not," said Rip. "The D.A. will have to advise you on that, but Ting can make a counterclaim for the labor involved."

"Ripley's right," McCaffery spoke up. "You better forget it, Charlie. You couldn't get a jury to decide it in your favor. You need Ting up there; he runs a fine commissary for you. My advice would be to make a deal with him and split the sweepings fifty-fifty in the future."

"Well, maybe you're right," Macgruder gave in testily. "I got rid of a bad headache, anyhow. Ripley. I don't want you to think I'm unappreciative of what you and your partner have done. Of course, if I had dreamed it was anything like this, I wouldn't have bothered to bring you out. You come up to the office in the morning and I'll have a check for you."

He excused himself and departed for the mountain.

Logan chuckled heartily.

"You took all the wind out of his sails, Rip! I never saw Charlie Macgruder left so flat. It's no wonder Mac and I couldn't make head nor tail out of his high-grading."

The partners lingered a few minutes. The afternoon train had arrived while they were in the courthouse. At the hotel, Grumpy glanced at the register and got a surprise. He hurried across the lobby to Rip, who had stopped to buy a newspaper.

"We didn't git done with that Midas job none too soon," said he.

"What do you mean?" Rainbow asked.

"Miss Greenwood's here! Her name's in the book. She musta jest got in."

Chapter Seven

THE ROUGH-DRAWN MAP

THE BARNLIKE PARLOR of the Union House, with its dust and faded furniture, was an almost forgotten part of the old hotel. Any business its guests might have was invariably transacted downstairs in the lobby.

Lane Greenwood was not aware of the gloominess of the room as she talked with Rainbow and Grumpy. Her surprise and delight at finding them in Wolf River was not easily overcome.

"I'm simply bewildered," she told them. "If anyone can help me, it's you. But I don't know how I shall ever be able to pay you."

"There won't be nothin' to pay for," the little one declared stoutly. "Yore pa was our friend. We're goin' to see this thing through, no matter how long it takes. Rip and me decided all that some time ago."

"It's so kind of you," Lane murmured. "Mr. McCaffery and Sheriff Logan have given me so much of their time that I can't blame them for being annoyed at my persistence. But I haven't changed my mind; I know my father was murdered."

"You've come to accept the fact that he's dead?" asked Rainbow.

Lane winced.

"What else can I think, Mr. Ripley? It's been so long now. I'm sorry I told Mr. Robbins I'd have dinner with him and Mrs. Robbins this evening. I have so much to say to you."

"We can get together tomorrow," said Rip. "And we

better find a place with a little more privacy than we have here."

"Have you become acquainted with Mr. Robbins?" she inquired.

"No, we haven't. We know Tom Stewart, the mayor, and a number of other men, but we kept away from Mr. Robbins deliberately. We understand he was your father's closest friend in Wolf River. For that reason, we felt we wanted to talk with you before we approached him."

"I was just thinking," said Lane, "that he would be glad to have us meet at his place tomorrow."

"I couldn't suggest anything better. What time shall we make it?"

"After the morning train arrives. Do you remember Del Blanchard?"

"Blanchard?" Grumpy repeated. "Ain't he the young fella we stumbled over outside your house, that night in Reno?"

Lane smiled.

"That was Del. Father placed him with the Candelaria Company on graduation. He's given up his position and is coming here to be with me. I expect him in the morning. I guess you must surmise that Del and I are engaged."

"Considering the way we met him, he struck us as a nice lad," said Rainbow. "It'll come in very handy to have a mining engineer with us. We won't keep you any longer now. We'll see you at Mr. Robbins's place about ten. And let me urge you to swear Perce Robbins to absolute secrecy before you discuss your father's case with him. You can tell him it's on our orders. He's a well-meaning but rather garrulous old man."

"He does like to talk," Lane admitted. "There isn't

anything he wouldn't do for me."

"I know—but talk is the very thing we want to avoid."

The evening was mild and pleasant. With nothing better to do, the partners strolled up and down the street. A low-hanging desert moon cast a charitable radiance over Wolf River and swept away most of its daytime ugliness. High on Midas Mountain, the stamp mills and smelter were sharply silhouetted against the great silvery orb.

"The Midas Company is the whole town," said Rip. "Without it, there'd be nothing here."

Grumpy nodded and did not break his train of thought. After they had passed the Silver Dollar, he propounded a startling question.

"Rip, is that gal safe in this town?"

"Well!" Rip exclaimed. "That's a surprising thing to say. It hadn't occurred to me that she was in any danger. Fools do strange things, but I can't believe anyone would harm her in the hope of heading off further investigation of her father's disappearance. That would only point it up. If anybody's in danger, we are—or very likely will be. We better start packing our guns tomorrow. If anybody's keeping cases on us, they'll know when they see us with Miss Greenwood and young Blanchard that we're taking a hand."

"I got ole Mary Ann on my hip right now," Grumpy confessed.

Blanchard arrived in the morning. He was present, with Lane and Perce, when the partners stepped into the assayer's office. After the introductions were over, Del said, "I hope this meeting will be pleasanter than our first. You only half believed what I said about those two men. But I was right; they were there for only one reason."

"There wouldn't seem to be much doubt of that now," the tall man agreed. "Suppose we sit here, where we can see anyone coming in. If we're interrupted, we'll say nothing further until we're alone again. We'll start with you, Miss Greenwood, and then we'll ask you a few questions, Mr. Robbins. The two of us have had long talks with the district attorney, the sheriff, and Mr. Blanton—he was in that country when your father was and just got out alive, we understand—so we needn't go over that part of it."

Rainbow hesitated, trying to find the right place to begin.

"I'm going to call you Lane," said he.

"I wish you would," she told him.

"Well, Lane, the first thing, I think, is the letter Moy Kim mailed to you. Do you have it with you?"

She had several papers in a heavy Manila envelope. She handed the letter to Rainbow. He read it, and so did Grumpy.

"No question but what yore pa figgered his search was jest about over," the doughty little man observed.

"Grumpy—do you and Rainbow doubt that he found the Lost Buckaroo?" Lane asked tensely.

It was Rip who answered.

"He found it, or he wouldn't have been killed. It's as simple as that, as we see it."

"Then you believe he was murdered?" Lane's voice trembled with the question.

"We do," replied Rainbow. "We've thought so from the first. But to go on. How did you discover, Lane, that Moy Kim bought two rifles and ammunition when he came back to Wolf River?"

"I canvassed every store in town. I have a list of everything he bought, even down to the amount of dried beans he got. Kim was in Chinatown that day, too."

"What luck did you have there?" asked Grumpy. "Do you know who he talked to?"

"He saw Quan Chew, the leader of the Wolf River Chinese, for one."

"Do you know what they talked about?"

"Only that Father had asked Kim to learn from Mr. Chew if William was working in the Monitors or Solomons with his Chinese prospectors."

Lane had to explain that William Chew had graduated from the Mackay School of Mines and his connection with her father.

"Mr. Chew told me William had been in the Monitors since early in June."

"Maybe he was," Del remarked skeptically. "I've given this a lot of thought, and I wonder if Willie Chew isn't the key to the whole thing."

Lane turned on him, aghast.

"Del, you can't mean that! William was always so grateful for Father's interest in him."

"Lane, that wouldn't mean a thing if the prize happened to be a mine worth millions."

"Young man, you're all wrong!" old Perce spoke up. "I've known Willie Chew since he was a boy. He's as straight as a ramrod!"

"I've got nothing against him," Del protested. "But he's shrewd; I know a lot of so-called mining engineers and geologists who can't hold a candle to him. I've heard Professor Greenwood say in a joke if he didn't find the Lost Buckaroo, Willie would."

The partners exchanged a glance. Del's suspicions struck them as groundless.

"Lane—you didn't mention Quan Chew to the district

attorney, did you?" Rip questioned.

"No, I thought it was unimportant at the time. I found something recently that proves how mistaken I was. Father and Kim were in the Solomons, Rainbow. They evidently knew they were being watched or followed. At least, they had seen someone. That's why Father wanted to know if it was William and his men they had caught sight of. Don't you see?"

"I think I do." Rainbow's tone was sober. "I regard it as about as important a bit of information as we possess. You say you found something recently that opened your eyes—"

"This," said Lane. "When I sold the furniture, I went through everything. I found it in Father's desk."

She handed Rip a rough, penciled map that showed a twisting S-shaped canyon. There were notations on it: *High conglomerate dike to left; steep wall on right.* Spanish Tanks was indicated. An arrow pointed to the southwest. Below it were the words *Five miles.* A circle had been drawn around a spot far down in the canyon, and it was marked *Here.*

Here meant the Lost Buckaroo. That was obvious enough, but it was equally true that Henry Greenwood could not have given the position of the mine on any map until he had found it, and this sketch had been made before he left Reno. It was reasoned conjecture on his part, nothing more.

Rainbow had no difficulty convincing them of the accuracy of this reasoning.

"But it's almost as important to us as though it were a map of the mine," he continued. "We know where to start looking now."

With his usual patience, Rip continued to question

Lane until it became apparent to him that she could tell them nothing further.

A messenger from the Midas Company came in for some work that Perce had finished. With the man's departure, Rip addressed himself to the old assayer.

"Yes," Perce answered, "I saw Henry Greenwood before he left Wolf River. He got in on the late-afternoon train and left for the desert by noon the next day. But he stopped in for half an hour almost as soon as he hit town. We didn't have much to say about the trip he was setting off on. He asked about William. I hadn't seen the boy in weeks, and I told Henry so. The fact of the matter is, I had a surprise for him, and we spent most of our time discussing it."

"What sort of a surprise?" came from Grumpy.

"An assay I had made for Cord Blanton. The two men he took a gamble on had brought in some samples. The formation was a strange one to me. All full of crystallized feldspar and black mica. You don't find that stuff in this part of Nevada."

"Tonopah, Goldfield, the Panamints," Del Blanchard volunteered.

"That's right," Perce agreed. "The stuff was good ore; about seventy dollars. I kept a piece and showed it to Henry. He couldn't believe it any more than I could, but when I suggested that these fellows had bootlegged the samples and were trying to take somebody for a sucker, he wouldn't believe it; he said Miller and McGarry would have to show Blanton something or he'd walk out on them. He called it a freak formation. I'll say it's a freak!"

Perce wagged his head scornfully.

"If there's a formation like that in the Monitors or Solomons, they'll have to show it to me before I'll believe it!

Those fellows are still pulling Blanton's leg. They got washed out on the first time in. Now they're talking about going in again this fall. I bet those birds light out for parts unknown at the last minute."

"If those gents are takin' Blanton over the ropes, that's his headache," Grumpy declared, and Rip agreed.

A thought occurred to both, however, and Rainbow put it into words.

"It could have been Blanton's party the professor saw."

"That's not what he claims," Perce returned. "He says they didn't see a soul."

"That may be the truth," said Rip. "The fact that they saw no one doesn't mean that someone didn't see them. We've often spotted men on our back trail without giving them a glimpse of us. There's something you said to Mr. McCaffery, Lane, that we want to keep in mind. Wolf River is only one of many points from which a man can jump off for the wastelands below Toquima Basin. It would be a mistake to go ahead on the theory that because your father went in from here the man, or men, who jumped him did likewise. The percentage would seem to be all against it."

"I dunno," Grumpy demurred. "Why do you say that, Rip?"

"Because I can't believe this job was committed by someone who just chanced to bump into the professor and Moy Kim. I think there was some long-time scheming behind it, based without doubt, on a more or less intimate knowledge of Henry Greenwood's plans. That being so, wouldn't this unknown party have been smart enough to realize it would be inviting suspicion to have any association with Wolf River? You see how Blanton's name keeps popping into our talk, and only because we know he was in that country in June. For no better reason, Blanchard is suspicious of young Chew. We haven't anything on either of them."

"You make yore point," the little one conceded. "But the trail is bound to lead to Wolf River sooner or later. This is the county seat. A man can't register minin' property anywhere else. McCaffery says no claims have been filed in that district of late. That doesn't mean somebody ain't waitin' till Miss Lane's father has been forgotten. That's providin' this Lost Buckaroo is somethin' more than a little ledge that ain't already been picked clean."

"You're wrong, Mr. Gibbs!" old Perce declared with some asperity. "No one's looted the Lost Buckaroo. It's a hardrock mine. The samples Johnnie Bidwell left with me are proof enough of that. I knew Johnnie well. From what he told me, I was able to make a graph of the vein. No, sir, gentlemen, the Lost Buckaroo hasn't been carted away by any desert rat!"

"I want to find my father—wherever he lies—and see the man who killed him brought to justice," said Lane. "The mine is a secondary consideration with me."

Rip and Grumpy were in sympathetic agreement with her, but they knew the first thing to be done was to run to earth whoever had killed Greenwood. That could hardly be accomplished without providing them with further information regarding the mine. It should be sufficient, coupled with the map Lane had found, to lead them to the Lost Buckaroo. On the other hand, it appeared altogether unlikely they would ever find any trace of Greenwood himself.

"We'll have to decide how best to go at it," said Rainbow. "Grumpy and I will work out something. It shouldn't take us more than a day or two. We'll have to get down into that country and stay there for some time."

"It'll take us longer than a couple days to git everythin' set," the little one argued. "First off, we'll have to git an experienced desert man to go with us—someone who really knows those mountains and who can use a gun in a pinch."

"Wild Bill Melody is your man," Perce asserted. "That's if you can get him to go. He's ratted all over this part of Nevada and knows it like a book. If he thought you were asking him into some gun trouble, I guess you could persuade him; Bill's that kind."

"By hickory, sounds like he was the man for us! Where do we find him?"

"He lives at his son's Seven Springs ranch, five, six miles east of town. You can find him there most any time."

To the partners' surprise, Lane told them she had hoped to engage Wild Bill to accompany Del and herself into the Solomons.

"I went to see him the last time I was in Wolf River," she continued. "He growled like an old bear when he heard what I wanted. He said he 'wa'n't takin' no female into them desert mountains.' Before I left, he'd halfway changed his mind. He agreed to think it over, at least. I'm sure that between us we can get him to agree to go with us. I'll be glad to pay him whatever he asks."

This was the first intimation the partners had that she intended to accompany them. Rainbow was instantly averse to it, and the little one was so filled with objections that he couldn't contain himself.

"*Jee*rusalem, honey, don't tell me yo're thinkin' of taggin' along with us! This ain't no pleasure trip we're goin' on! The rats that stopped yore pa will shore try to stop us!"

"Lane, that's just good sense," Rip said firmly. "Give up any thought of going with us."

"Please, Rainbow!" she pleaded earnestly. "Don't leave me behind! I'm young and strong; I can stand the trip. Whatever danger there is, I insist on sharing it with you. I won't slow you up; Del can look after me, and I can do the cooking, if nothing else."

The tall man shook his head.

"I appreciate your courage and unselfishness, but it would be a mistake to let you go. It'll be a few days before we pull out; the picture may change before then, but unless it changes radically, I'll have to say no."

Cleve Miller strolled by as they sat there. He looked in. He had been watching the place for some time. His curiosity had been aroused when he saw Lane and Del leave the hotel. He was in no doubt as to who she was, having seen her in Wolf River on her previous visits. A glance at the hotel register supplied him with Del Blanchard's name and the fact that he was from Reno.

Del's romantic interest in Lane was obvious enough to supply the reason for his presence in town. Miller promptly forgot about him. It was quite another story with the partners and Lane. He knew why they were conferring at such length, and it didn't ease his anxiety to have Perce Robbins sitting in with them.

After passing the assayer's office, he stopped in front of the hardware store, two doors away. Leaning against one of the posts that held up the wooden awning, he built himself a cigarette and riveted his attention on the little frame building Perce occupied.

Cleve had been standing there some minutes when a young, completely Americanized Chinese swung past him and turned in at Robbins's office.

"Hunh!" Miller muttered to himself. "That's young Chew! This is a real powwow, with the Chinks getting into it!"

He held all Chinese in contempt, but a cold chill ran down his spine as he heard the door close on William Chew. He knew Chinese prospectors had been delving into the Monitors and Solomons all summer. Had one of them uncovered a clue to Greenwood's disappearance?

You can be damned sure it's somethin'! Cleve thought. *That young punk ain't in there to discuss the time of day!*

Chew had returned from his long sojourn in the wastelands earlier in the week. He had gone to the house of his father, Quan Chew, at once. Lum Duck, the gold dealer and head of the Chinese mining co-operative, had been called in to discuss a matter of the gravest import. For two days he had debated the question with his honorable father and Lum Duck. A decision had been arrived at only this morning, and it was in keeping with it that he was in town now, seeking Rainbow.

He knew the partners were in Wolf River. He had also been informed that Lane and Del Blanchard were here. The dispatch with which news of that sort was carried over the hill to Chinatown would have surprised the community. In quite the same way, Rip would have been surprised had he known how well-acquainted Chew was with him, even though they had never met.

"Hello, William!" Lane greeted the young man warmly. "It's nice to see you again."

"Thank you, Miss Greenwood. May I extend my sympathy to you? You know how I admired your father."

He had a nod for Del and bowed to Rainbow and Grumpy as Lane introduced them.

"I can hardly regard you as a stranger, Mr. Ripley,"

said William. "I know you wear the ring of the family of Seng. I am of that family; Mei-lang is my cousin. I have often heard her speak of you. And of you, Mr. Gibbs."

"This is indeed a most pleasant surprise," Rainbow told him. "Your name was mentioned just a few minutes ago, so we don't feel unacquainted with you either. Won't you sit down?"

"No, thank you. And please forgive my intrusion, Mr. Ripley. May I ask a favor, sir? Will you and Mr. Gibbs honor the house of my father with your presence this evening? There's a certain matter on which we should like to have your advice, if you'd be so kind."

"Certainly," the tall man replied without hesitation. "It will be a pleasure. We are so seldom privileged to repay in even a small measure the many favors we have received from Miss Seng. Shall we say eight o'clock?"

Though he had no idea of the nature of the matter which William and his father desired to discuss with Grumpy and him, Rip's long experience with the Chinese warned him that it would not prove to be unimportant, for it was not their way to consult white men, however friendly, about their trivial concerns.

"Eight o'clock will be most convenient," said William. After thanking Rip, he spoke to Lane, telling her he hoped to see her again while she was in Wolf River. And to Del he said, "I understand you got your degree in June. Let me congratulate you. The last time I talked with Professor Greenwood he mentioned how well you were doing."

"He must have had somebody else in mind." Blanchard's tone was less than friendly. It wasn't because he bore any racial prejudice against William that he refused to unbend; there was a suspicion in his mind and he could not overcome it.

"What have you been doing, Willie?"

It was a leading question. If William found it embarrassing, he gave no sign of it.

"I've been prospecting in the Monitors and Solomon Mountains all summer," he said frankly. "It was very interesting." He turned to Rainbow apologetically. "I must not take any more of your time now."

He opened the door.

"I'll be expecting you about eight, Mr. Ripley. Just ask anyone; they will direct you to my father's house."

Cleve Miller, still lounging in front of the hardware store, caught those last words. They carried a sinister significance to him.

"They know something, or they wouldn't be getting together for another talkfest in Chinatown!" he snarled under his breath.

He made his way back to the Silver Dollar at once. Cord was out, but Pat McGarry sat at one of the tables.

"What's eatin' you?" McGarry demanded. "You're steamed about somethin'!"

"I'll say I am!" Cleve growled. "Cord says all we got to do is sit tight! We keep on doing that and we'll wake up some morning with a rope around our necks!"

Pat McGarry's hard-bitten face grew rockier than ever as he listened to what Miller had to say.

"You're dead right; they've turned up somethin'!" he agreed. "The sooner we stop them gents, the better off we'll be!"

"That's what I been telling Cord, but he won't listen! He's too damned smart for his own good, Pat!"

"He'll listen!" McGarry ground out grimly. "Either he'll do somethin' or we will!"

Chapter Eight

CADAVERS IN A CELLAR

THERE WERE NO SIDEWALKS in Wolf River's Chinatown. Its streets, just beaten paths, dusty in summer and ankle-deep with slush and mud in the spring when the snow was going off, meandered uncertainly along the slope overlooking the big wash, with little or no regard for a building line.

Rainbow and Grumpy had observed it in its sun-bleached drabness by day and found it the counterpart of other Nevada Chinatowns they had known. With the coming of nightfall, it took on color and life; the drabness faded, and a strange Oriental quaintness settled on the quarter.

This evening the paper lanterns suspended in front of the dozen or more shops bobbed in the wind. From the shop windows came the faint radiance of lights within. Men and women and children sat in the doorways, the singsong of their voices all but drowning out the melancholy notes of a flute player who sat at an open second-story window above a fan-tan parlor.

Rainbow caught the little one glancing back over his shoulder.

"You're spooky tonight," the tall man remarked. "That's the fourth time you've done that since we started over the hill."

"I jest wanta be shore we ain't bein' followed," Grumpy responded. "I don't mind usin' my neck when I figger it may save my head."

Rip smiled.

"It won't hurt a bit for both of us to keep our eyes open," said he.

They reached the main street of the quarter a few minutes later and were directed to the house of Quan Chew. It was a two-story brick building, one of the most substantial in Chinatown, and originally meant to be used as a general store. The lower floor had since been partitioned off, and the front room served as the office in which William's father conducted his private banking business.

A wooden porch extended across the width of the store, the floor of it only a step off the ground. The window shades were drawn, but the partners could see that a light burned within. The door opened as they reached it, and William invited them to enter. They saw him lock the door after they were admitted.

The furnishings of the office were old and simple. At one side of the room heavy iron grillwork formed an enclosure in which stood a large safe. A desk and a number of chairs completed the arrangement.

Two elderly Chinese sat at the desk. One of them was Lum Duck, the gold merchant. The partners correctly surmised that the other was Quan Chew.

"This is my father," said William. "Lum Duck you know."

Quan bowed with great dignity.

"My poor house is doubly honored by your presence, gentlemen. We know, from one whose advice we treasure, that we may rely on your understanding and friendly interest in our people to help us out of this difficulty. If you were not received more graciously yesterday afternoon, when you visited Lum Duck, may I say it was only because we surmised you had come on a far more important matter than a few grains of gold from Midas Mountain?"

"We should have taken you into our confidence at once," William spoke up. "I returned to Wolf River on Monday evening. When I learned you were here, I wanted to go to you immediately. I was not permitted to do so."

"My son is very young," Quan Chew observed weightily. "He is not unaware of the contempt and prejudice with which white men regard even the most learned of us; but he knows nothing of the hatred and injustice which his elders have suffered. You know what our lot has been, gentlemen—cheated, despoiled, murdered, the law misused to punish but never to protect us." He shook his head solemnly. "The record makes one cautious. If any harm has been done by not getting in touch with you sooner, I am willing to accept the responsibility."

It struck a decidedly serious note. The demeanor of old Lum Duck reflected it eloquently. Even young William's manner was enormously sober. What all this was leading up to was a mystery to the partners.

Quan Chew spoke to his son in his native Chinese. William replied briefly and turned to Rainbow.

"My father feels that we should inform you before anything further is said that it was at the insistence of Seng Mei-lang that he and Lum Duck agreed to take you and Mr. Gibbs into our confidence."

Rip did not attempt to conceal his surprise at having Mei-lang's name brought into the conversation.

"You have been in communication with Miss Seng by mail?" he inquired.

"My father telegraphed her soon after my return, requesting her to come to Wolf River at once. She has been here since yesterday morning."

The tall man threw off the shock of it and regarded

William and the two elderly Chinese intently.

"Am I to understand that Miss Seng requested us to be here this evening?"

"Yes, Mr. Ripley," the young man replied. "She is waiting for us upstairs. Before we join her, there is something in the cellar I wish you to see. There is an inside stairway in back. I left a lantern burning. Shall we go?"

Grumpy caught Rip's eye and flashed him a glance that registered his disapproval of the proceedings. The tall man nodded; he wanted an explanation, too, before going any further.

"William, we took it for granted, when you spoke to us this morning, that you and your father had something of a serious nature to discuss with us. What you've said this evening more than proves it. I gather that you are in trouble, and it must be serious indeed to have brought Miss Seng all the way up from San Francisco. I think it's time we were told what this is all about."

Quan Chew answered him.

"Mr. Ripley, if you and Mr. Gibbs will accompany my son to the cellar, you will be able to judge for yourselves how serious is the difficulty he has so innocently placed us in. We then will be able to discuss with Seng Mei-lang what is to be done."

Grumpy was about to object, but Rip silenced him with a glance, and they followed William to the rear of the store. When the young Chinese picked up a lighted kerosene lantern and continued down the stairs, Grumpy held back.

"Mebbe this is all right, and mebbe it ain't!" he muttered suspiciously. "We don't know what we're walkin' into! All we got for it is their word that Miss Seng is here!"

"If that's the way you feel, keep your hand on your gun," Rainbow advised, under his breath.

William held up his lantern to light the way. Rip joined him, and the little one followed, alert and cautious.

The cellar was littered with discarded furniture and a miscellaneous assortment of mining and garden tools. There was a stench in the air that was no part of the room's dankness. The cobwebs hanging from the beams and festooning the small windows seemed to indicate that the place was seldom entered.

A long wooden table stood in the center of the room. On it reposed two canvas-wrapped bundles. William walked to the table and hung the lantern on a nail in one of the beams.

"Mr. Ripley, this isn't a pretty sight I am about to show you," said he, "but it is necessary. I know you and Mr. Gibbs have seen dead men before."

Lifting a corner of the canvas on the bundle nearest him, he threw it back, revealing the mutilated and badly decomposed body of a huge man, still identified as Chinese.

"Good God!" Grumpy exclaimed. "That's terrible! Looks like the coyotes and buzzards had been feedin' on him!"

Understanding began to flash through Rainbow. His gray eyes narrowed as they fastened on young Chew.

"William—this is Moy Kim! I recognize his gold teeth."

"It is Kim," William agreed. "There never has been any question of it in my mind. We found certain trinkets of his near the body. But I wanted you to be convinced, Mr. Ripley. If—"

"Hold on a minute!" Grumpy growled. He indicated the other bundle with a jerk of his head. "Is that Greenwood you got there?"

"I shall let you decide for yourselves," said Chew.

He threw back the tarp, exposing the broken and mutilated body of a white man. Rip was the first to speak.

"It's Henry Greenwood."

William nodded gravely.

"When he was in the field, Professor Greenwood always wore his watch attached to his belt. He still wears it, Mr. Ripley. I wish you would examine it."

It was a hunting-case watch. Rainbow opened it and found a name engraved on the hinged cover.

" 'Henry A. Greenwood,' " he read aloud. "That settles it, Grump!"

"It settles the fact that he's dead but it don't settle nothin' else in my mind! You want to begin talkin', young fella!" the little man advised Chew. "Where'd you find these men? And how?"

The hostility in his tone did not escape William.

"If it were not my intention to give you a full explanation of everything, Mr. Gibbs, you would not be here now," he observed pointedly. "The circumstances are such that I knew I couldn't hope to escape the suspicion of some men, but I hardly expected to find you doubting me, even before I have had a chance to speak."

"Strikes me you've had chances galore to do some talkin'," the little one returned. "Keepin' a couple dead men down here in this cellar for three, four days is mighty peculiar, to say the least. Cover 'em up and let's hear what's on your mind!"

"Take it easy, Grump," Rainbow advised. "You've been on the peck all evening." He turned to William. "I don't know what you have to say, but you and your men brought the bodies in. It stands to reason that if you had been involved in any way, you would have left them where you found them."

Young Chew thanked him.

"It is true that we brought them in. Moy Kim was one of us; we wanted him to be buried according to our customs. As for Professor Greenwood, I owe him so much that leaving him to lie in an unmarked grave would have been the basest ingratitude. Even though I had known then what I know now, I wouldn't have done differently. I know what I've let myself in for. This morning, when Del Blanchard asked me what I had been doing, I had only to say I'd been in the Solomons to see your heads go up; I realized immediately that you knew it was in those mountains that Professor Greenwood had lost his life."

"William, let us not misunderstand one another," Rip protested. "It is true we had traced Greenwood to the Solomons. It was a coincidence that you were there, too. Naturally, it surprised us to have you say so. I don't believe for a moment that you had anything to do with the deaths of these men. Will you let me put some questions to you? It may save time."

"I'll be glad to answer as best I can," Chew agreed. "It was my father's thought that I should acquaint you with all the facts, in order that Seng Mei-lang might be spared some of the grim details. What is your first question, Mr. Ripley?"

"William, when Moy Kim returned to Wolf River for additional supplies, he saw your father at Greenwood's request and was told that you were then working in the Monitors."

"That was the truth, sir. We didn't leave the Monitors

until two weeks ago. We had found several small deposits of gold. We took out everything we could and then moved on. You and Mr. Gibbs know that is our custom. In the type of desert mining we do, it is seldom worth while to register a claim. We covered a lot of territory. By the first of September, I felt we might do better if we crossed the lower basin to the Solomons. We knew Lum Duck's messengers would be arriving with fresh supplies shortly. We waited for them and then struck off to the west. We reached Spanish Tanks two days later."

"You mind tellin' us where Lum Duck fits into this?" Grumpy broke in.

"We have a syndicate through which all of our mining activities are conducted," the young Chinese answered. "Lum Duck directs it. We had as many as twenty men in the field this summer. My party of four was the only one working south of Toquima Basin."

"You knew, of course, that Professor Greenwood was in that country?" said Rainbow.

William nodded in the affirmative.

"Lum Duck had sent the information to me. The season was getting late; I knew the professor would have to be back in Reno soon. I didn't know exactly where he was or what luck he had had, but while we were camped at Spanish Tanks, I expressed the hope that we might run into him on his way out. I had no premonition of how soon I was to see him, or that I was to find him dead."

"How far is it from Spanish Tanks into the Solomons?" the tall man inquired.

"To the upper Solomons—about five, maybe six miles. They rise out of the desert precipitately, behind a long, unbroken porphyry dike that stands out like a protecting barrier reef. The Solomons themselves are a maze of canyons. I had never seen them before, but two of my men knew the range. It was during the afternoon of the day we left Spanish Tanks that I got the first intimation that disaster of some sort had befallen Professor Greenwood."

"What was it?" Grumpy demanded. The straightforwardness of the young man's story had begun to impress him.

"One of my men, Wah Chang, called my attention to something moving across the desert in our direction. In a few minutes, we realized it was a burro. The animal was so weak it could barely move. It would take a step or two and stop. Several times it dropped to its knees. It stumbled once more, while we were still some distance away. It tried to struggle to its feet but couldn't make it. As you know, we never use burros; we prefer the two-wheeled cart. It's often slow, hard work pushing them through the sand. I don't know how long it took us to reach the burro, but it was dead when we did. It had starved to death; it was just skin and bones."

"Do you mean to say you recognized it as one of Greenwood's burros?" asked Rainbow.

"Not at all," young Chew replied. "We unbuckled the empty packsaddle the burro had been dragging. The little fellow was so thin that the saddle had slipped off its back. Burned in the wooden saddletree with a stenciling-iron was the owner's name—H. A. Greenwood. I have the saddle here, if you care to examine it."

"No, I prefer to have you continue with your story," said Rip. "You knew Greenwood was in trouble. What did you do?"

"It was not difficult to follow the tracks the burro had made. I considered that the logical thing to do. They led us into a long, twisting canyon. We saw evidence almost at once that a mighty torrent had swept through it some-time during the summer. Stains on the canyon walls showed us the height the water had reached. Cloudbursts had been severe in the Monitors, but we had seen nothing like this; a blanket of sand, three to four feet deep in places, had been deposited by the flood waters. The wheels of the carts sank in the fresh sand, and we made very little progress—not more than two miles by night-fall. Chang and I went ahead on foot, next morning, try-ing to find a way to get the carts through. We had gone only a short distance when we saw buzzards rising. They circled overhead, waiting for us to pass. We knew they were feeding on something. Chang found it—a human arm, protruding from the sand, and stripped to the bone."

William shook his head, as though trying to throw off the memory of it.

"It was Moy Kim," he continued a moment later. "Less than a hundred yards away we found Professor Green-wood. I called the others, and we dug the bodies out of the sand and wrapped them in the canvas covers we use on the carts. I didn't question but what the professor and Kim had been caught in the canyon and drowned when the cloudburst broke. It seemed obvious that the torrent had swept them along for miles and buried them where we found them. I didn't try to find their camp; I was sure there was nothing left of it. We had expected to spend at least a month in the Solomons. Chang and the others agreed with me that we'd have to call off our plans and start for Wolf River at once."

He caught Grumpy shaking his head dubiously. The perplexed look in Rainbow's eyes was equally disturbing to him.

"Mr. Ripley, is it possible you and Mr. Gibbs doubt

the truth of what I have said?" he asked bluntly.

"Not a bit, William," the tall man replied. "I believe you've given us the truth as far as you've gone. It leaves us all at sea. From the first, it's been impossible for us to believe that Greenwood and Kim lost their lives in a cloudburst. I hardly know what to say to you."

"Let me finish, then," the young man said. "We made excellent time getting back. I knew the authorities would have to be notified. It was my intention to see Sheriff Logan the next morning. The first thing to be done, however, was to call in Doctor Soong to perform a postmortem; we knew we'd have to have a death certificate before we could bury Moy Kim. Doctor Soong came at once. He examined both bodies. It was only then that we discovered where we stood."

"What do you mean?" demanded Rainbow.

"Mr. Ripley—Doctor Soong proved to us that Professor Greenwood and Moy Kim were shot to death. They didn't die by drowning. He says they were dead when they fell, or were tossed, in the water."

"Wal!" the little one burst out triumphantly. "We had this business sized up correctly, after all!"

Rip had nothing to say. Whatever personal satisfaction he felt at having their contention confirmed was far less important to him than being able to confront the district attorney and the sheriff with positive proof that Greenwood and his companion had come to their deaths by gunfire.

The tall man was careful not to let his enthusiasm run away with him; he realized that, as yet, he had only an unknown Chinese physician's word for it that such evidence could be produced.

"This Doctor Soong," he said, "is he competent to perform an autopsy?"

"He should be." William smiled inscrutably. "He's a graduate of the University of California and did his post-graduate work at Columbia."

"That puts me in my place," said Rainbow. "Forgive me for not knowing better. In view of the condition the bodies are in, I presume an accurate autopsy was extremely difficult. Did Doctor Soong say how long ago he thought death had occurred?"

"Approximately ten weeks. That would place it early in July. Establishing the cause of death was not as difficult as you suggest, Mr. Ripley. You will want to talk to Doctor Soong, of course, but if you and Mr. Gibbs will step closer to the table, I can convince you it was a rifle slug that killed Professor Greenwood."

He took down the lantern and held it so that its yellow light revealed a leaden pellet lodged between the exposed fifth and sixth cervical vertebrae.

"That's enough for me," Grumpy muttered grimly. "That one slug would have done the trick!"

He turned his back to the table, anxious to be done with this grisly business.

Rip was not to be hurried. He asked William to move the lantern a few inches to the left.

"There!" said he. "No question about it; that bullet broke his neck."

The passage of time and the scavengers had long since made it impossible to say how it had entered the throat.

"One thing is sure," the tall man asserted. "The slug was pretty well spent when it hit him. It must have been fired at three to four hundred yards. That's something to remember. Have you anything further to say, William?"

Whether by accident or design, young Chew had not

mentioned the Lost Buckaroo.

The young Chinese glanced at Rip furtively and quick-ly pulled his eyes away. After a moment's hesitation, he said, "No. We can go up now."

He knows more than he's told us, thought Rainbow.

William covered the bodies and led the way to the stairs. He had taken only a step or two when he stopped in his tracks, his eyes riveted on a rear window.

"What is it?" Rip demanded.

"That window—I thought I saw two men there!"

"White men?"

"I—I thought so." William was so badly shaken he could barely speak. "Could someone have followed you to Chinatown?"

"Come on!" Grumpy cried, whipping out his gun. "Let's git out there and see what this is all about!"

"It's too late for that," Rainbow rapped. "If there was anyone at the window, they got an eyeful."

"Let's stop guessin' about it!" the little one growled. "I know there's no one there now, but we can see whether there was or not! Fetch the lantern!"

They found numerous footprints in the deep dust out-side the cellar window. Grumpy read them carefully.

"Two men, all right, and they was here some time, judgin' by the way the ground's cut up. They was wearin' heavy-heeled shoes. That spells white men to me!"

It drew a confirming nod from Rip.

"No question about it in my mind. We were followed, Grump. Whoever killed Greenwood is right here in Wolf River, and he's putting the finger on us. I would have liked to have held back what we learned tonight for a day or two, but that isn't possible now; the cat's out of the bag and we'll have to play it that way."

"You—think we are in danger, Mr. Ripley?" William asked anxiously.

"You bet we are! I'm surprised an attempt wasn't made to kill us in the cellar."

Chapter Nine

DESPERATE MEN

STEADY EMPLOYMENT, AT GOOD WAGES, in the mines on Midas Mountain had lured men to Wolf River from all over Nevada. The economic ups and downs of the calling they followed kept the great majority of them moving from one part of the state to another. A few were drifters by choice, "fiddlefoots," who never remained anywhere more than a month or two, whether a camp was booming or fading.

Since Cord Blanton had taken over the Silver Dollar, he had renewed acquaintance with at least half a dozen of these birds of passage, whom he had known in Tonopah, Las Vegas, and other towns. Two of them, Hank Buckout and Bill Kumler by name, aroused his interest. Knowing something about their past endeavors, he surmised they were in Wolf River, putting in ten hours a day at hard labor, only because they had found themselves in difficulty with the law somewhere in the southern part of the state.

Cord neither invited their confidence, nor became too friendly with them. He told himself, nevertheless, that if he ever needed them he had only to make them a proposition and they would throw up their jobs in a minute.

Buckout and Kumler were standing at the bar tonight. Blanton exchanged a word or two with them. It had been a trying day for him.

"I could handle that pair better than two damn half-wits I'm tied up with!" he grumbled to himself as he moved away.

He had wrangled with Cleve and McGarry for an hour that morning. It did not disturb him particularly to learn that Lane Greenwood was back in Wolf River and had been conferring with the two detectives. The Chinese angle held graver connotations in his mind. But, in any event, he didn't propose to be stampeded into opening up and showing his hand.

Blanton had no scruples against rubbing out the partners. It was the sheer idiocy of such a move that made him oppose it so violently. Cleve's threat that Pat and he were ready to take matters into their own hands unless something were done left Blanton unmoved; they were helpless without him, and he made them realize it.

He knew they were in Chinatown tonight, following Ripley and his partner. He had agreed to it, but only on their solemn promise not to lift a finger against the partners.

It was not yet nine o'clock when Cleve and McGarry slipped into the Silver Dollar by way of the rear entrance. The door to Cord's office stood open. He was not there.

"Up in front," Cleve muttered. "I'll get him. You wait here!"

He caught Blanton's eye. It brought the latter hurrying back.

"Come on in and shut the door!" Cleve jerked out.

Cord looked them over carefully.

"What the hell's happened to you?" he rapped. "You look scared to death!" His face was suddenly rocky. "You gave me your word you wouldn't use your guns! If you've double-crossed me, I'll—"

"Forget it!" Pat growled. "We didn't put a finger on our guns, and it's too damned bad we didn't, and you'll say so when you hear what we've got to say!"

"Well?"

"Cord—they got Greenwood and the Chink in the cellar of Quan Chew's house. We saw the bodies! Saw everythin'! That's what they brought Ripley and Gibbs down to see!"

Blanton had to brace himself.

"You sure?" he demanded fiercely.

"You bet we're sure!" Miller told him. "We saw it all through a cellar window. Ripley identified Greenwood's watch. You know what shape those stiffs are in, after all this time. Make you sick to look at 'em. Greenwood's watch was fastened to his belt. Ripley had to examine it to be sure it really was him."

"Could you hear what they were saying?" Blanton's voice was rough as a file.

"We caught a word or two—that was all. They dug 'em up somewheres. What the hell difference does it make where or how? I tell you, Cord, this is the showdown! You've had everything your way up to now, and this is where it's got us! We're in the soup, and you know it!"

Blanton sat down heavily.

"We got to think this thing out," he muttered.

"That's what you been doin' a long time—thinkin' it out!" McGarry snarled. "Those two birds are still down in Chinatown. If we got any sense, we'll nail 'em on their way over the hill!"

"You talk like fools!" Cord shot back. "Do you think killing the two of them will stop this? What about the Chinks? How many of them do you figure are in the know? If you got any brains, start using them!"

He reminded them how they had leaped to the conclusion that Rainbow and the little one were in Wolf River on the Greenwood matter, when they first arrived.

"You know better now! You're making an even bigger mistake this time! To listen to you, we're due to be arrested in a few minutes! What nonsense! I tell you we ain't under no suspicion. Let 'em produce the bodies. That don't tie a thing on us—not if we continue to sit tight. It takes nerve to stand pat when the chips are down. If you guys have got any guts, this is the time to show it."

"You mean we're going to wait and let this thing smack us right in the face?" Cleve demanded incredulously.

"We're going to wait till it breaks—that's what I mean!" Cord said flatly. "Ripley and his partner can't hold back more'n a day or two. There'll be some excitement when the news comes out that Greenwood is officially dead and the Lost Buckaroo is still anybody's property who can locate it. Willie Chew will have to state where he found the bodies. When he does, it'll start a stampede for the Solomons. That'll give us the chance we want; while the rest of the town's still talking about going after the mine, we'll be organized and on our way. We'll hire somebody like old Wild Bill Melody to take us in. We don't need him, but that'll make it look better. And we won't make no secret of what we're after; we'll tell Ripley and the rest that we're going to find the Lost Buckaroo. Do you begin to get me?"

Cleve nodded skeptically.

"That sounds all right but for one thing. Logan is going to be called in, and McCaffery and the coroner. Suppose they discover that Greenwood and the Chinaman stopped some lead? Where's that going to leave us?"

"How they going to find out anything like that?" Cord demanded scornfully. "It's been too long. You say you saw the bodies. Is there anything left of them?"

"Damn little," McGarry answered. "Clothes ripped to

ribbons. Looked to me like the coyotes and buzzards had been workin' on 'em. I bet that's how the Chinks found 'em."

"So do I!" Blanton agreed. "If Ripley had to look at Greenwood's watch to identify him, we got nothing to worry about. But I'm warning you, don't start putting our outfit together till I give the word. The two of you begin at the beginning now and tell me just what happened after you went over the hill tonight."

They had followed the partners to Chinatown and seen them enter the house of Quan Chew. After a few minutes, the appearance of a light in the cellar had drawn them to the rear window. Their detailed account of what they had observed was both complete and graphic. Blanton found nothing in it to cause him to change his plans.

The more carefully he contemplated the move he had outlined, the better he liked it. He had intended to allow the coming fall and winter to pass before startling Wolf River with the announcement that he and his partners had found the Lost Buckaroo. There'd be no need to wait now. Better still, they could forget about the alleged strike Pat and Miller had made.

They talked it over at length.

"This will work out all right for us," he told them. "It'll even be better than what we figured on. Thank God we kept our mouths shut and didn't do a thing. I knew that was the way to play it! We get a break and we're in position to take advantage of it!"

Having convinced himself that this was so, he managed to instill a measure of confidence in them. Their complacency would have received a rude jar, however, had they been aware that the partners had a double reason for their presence in the Chinese quarter tonight.

By arrangement, Mei-lang had left the train at the station north of Wolf River, where she had found William waiting for her with a carriage. Without attracting attention, she had reached the house of his father.

Less than four months had passed since Rainbow had seen her last, in Star City. He found her more lovely than ever, if that were possible. Her pride and unassailable dignity rested on her as gracefully tonight as ever.

Usually, they had met unexpectedly and in varied circumstances, some of them ugly and dangerous. He had never known her to waver either in her courage or unselfish devotion to her people.

There was nothing about the exterior of the house of Quan Chew to suggest the rich luxury to be found in his living-room. With its brocaded hangings, framed embroideries and hand-carved teakwood furniture inlaid with mother-of-pearl, it formed a perfect background for Seng Mei-lang's exquisite beauty. This evening she wore the traditional black of the high-caste Chinese woman, her sheathlike sleeveless gown revealing the slim perfection of her figure. She was faultlessly groomed, as always.

Rainbow was flattered to find her wearing the jade earrings he had given her.

"Did you know that we were in Wolf River?" he asked, after they had spoken for several minutes.

"No, it came as a very pleasant surprise. It was my intention to wire you after I had talked with Chew Quan." She inverted the name, according to Chinese custom. "Fortunately, that wasn't necessary. But I still must trespass on our friendship, Rainbow, and ask your assistance. I'm sure you realize by now what the situation is."

"I'm not sure that I do," said Rip. "William appears to fear the consequences of what he has done; he speaks of the difficulty he's in. His father and Lum Duck seem to be even more concerned."

The two elderly Chinese nodded gravely.

"The difficulty they see is with the law, I take it," Rainbow continued. "From what I've been told, I don't know of any reason why they should be so alarmed. Bringing in the bodies was a humane thing to do. Keeping them in the cellar for three or four days was a mistake."

"I explained all that to you, Mr. Ripley," William spoke up. "After Doctor Soong found that Professor Greenwood and Moy Kim had been killed by gunfire, I was afraid to go to the authorities. We didn't know what to do. It was then that my father sent for Seng Mei-lang."

The tall man shook his head. He knew Grumpy and he had yet to hear the whole story.

"I'm afraid the district attorney will find that a very unsatisfactory explanation," said he. "I know of no reason why you should have feared going to him at once. Surely that was Doctor Soong's duty."

Mei-lang studied his lean, sober face with her dark, intelligent eyes.

"If I didn't know you so well, I would think we were playing at cross-purposes," she remarked, with a faint trace of annoyance. "I'm sure you understand as fully as I do why my cousin hesitated about going to the district attorney. He is a Chinese, a mining engineer. He and his party were in the Solomons looking for gold; Professor Greenwood was in those same mountains, seeking a lost mine. Now, William and his men return to Wolf River with the bullet-riddled bodies of the professor and Moy Kim. How long do you think it will be after that becomes known before suspicion will be running wild against him?"

"There'll be some talk," Rainbow admitted. "I'd expect that, in any event. But I'm sure you're unduly alarmed—unless there's more to this than we've been told."

Though the remark was pointed enough to call for an answer, Mei-lang ignored it. As for the Chews and Lum Duck, their faces remained completely impassive.

"I'm sure I am not overstating the case," she said. "The cry will go up that Professor Greenwood found the Lost Buckaroo and that the Chinese killed him and have his secret locked away against the day when it will be safe to start working the mine. You know how far this senseless hatred and prejudice can go. You need evidence when you accuse a white man; suspicion is enough to convict one of us. In my work for the China Society, I've seen it happen too often not to know how true it is."

"I can't deny that," Rip countered. "But even suspicion has to have something on which to feed. I can't see anything for it to get its teeth in. The Greenwood case interests us in more ways than one. Grumpy and I are going to stick with it to the finish."

He told her of their friendship with the professor and the promise they had given Lane to bring her father's murderers to justice.

"If we can work together," he continued, "you can be of as much—or more—help to us than we can be to you."

"That's if we can work together, Miss Seng," the little one echoed. "We'll have to put all our cards on the table."

His tone said plainly enough that he was of the opinion it hadn't been done, up to now. Rip voiced his complete agreement with him.

"We're dealing with desperate men, and the chips are down right now," said he. "Make no mistake about that."

Chapter Ten

To Smoke Out the Rats—

MEI-LANG'S HEAD WENT UP ever so slightly. It was a disturbing moment for her. She met it, however, with a dissembling smile.

"I'm sorry, gentlemen. I took it for granted that we would work together. Is it possible you doubt William's story?"

"No—not up to a certain point," Rainbow said firmly. "But there's a lot that's been left unsaid. If I had no other reason to think so, the very fact that you are here would be enough in itself to convince me that something far more urgent than the fear you express that William may be suspected of the crime is responsible for your presence. I'm sure I can tell you what it is."

"Very well, proceed," Mei-lang challenged coolly.

Rainbow had the feeling that the Chews and Lum Duck were hanging on his words.

"I'm sure what you all are so concerned about is the Lost Buckaroo," he said thoughtfully. He kept an eye on William, believing that of the four, he would be most likely to betray some sign of surprise or dismay. He was rewarded by seeing the young Chinese draw in his breath sharply. "Downstairs, and again while we were in the cellar," he went on, "no mention was made of the mine. The omission was so noticeable that I began to realize it wasn't by accident that the subject was being so carefully

avoided. According to William, he didn't think it important to discover where the Professor and Kim had been
caught by the cloudburst. He says the flood may have carried the bodies several miles down the canyon. On the
face of it, that couldn't be true; it was only a flash flood,
raging for a few minutes. Considering the experience he's
had with cloudbursts in that country, I'm sure he realized
at once that he had only to go on for a half to three-
quarters of a mile to reach the spot where he believed
Henry Greenwood and Moy Kim had been trapped."

Mei-lang knew he wasn't finished. The pulse in her
throat beat faster as she waited for him to continue.

"William was fully acquainted with Greenwood's
search for the Lost Buckaroo. As a young mining engineer, and quite apart from every other consideration, I'm
sure he found the urge to discover whether the professor
had located the mine before he met his death utterly ir-
resistible. He had nothing to hold him back, no thought
of danger, for he honestly believed the two men had been
drowned."

"And you conclude from that that he found the mine?"

Seng Mei-lang regarded him with an obscure interest.
Neither from her tone nor the expression on her delicate-
ly sculptured face could her reaction to what he was saying be judged.

"I do," said Rainbow. "I've heard his professional abil-
ity spoken of so highly that I'm sure he didn't get that
close to it and miss it. It's obvious by now that the Lost
Buckaroo lies in that canyon, that Greenwood found it
and was jumped soon after he did. We don't know who
killed him and Moy Kim. We know it wasn't William
and his party. If any proof of that were necessary, the
fact that we were spied on tonight would supply it."

"We can go further than that," Grumpy declared, breaking his long silence. "It's plain enough to me that the gents who knocked off the professor and Moy Kim figgered the smart play was to leave the mine untouched for a few months. It'd been sittin' there for years without bein' found. They musta argued from that that it'd be safe there a while longer. We know they ain't workin' the mine or they wouldn't be in Wolf River keepin' cases on us. I reckon they been here some time."

"I'm sure they have," said Rip. "I believe they got out of the Solomons as quickly as they could. Otherwise, William would have had quite a different story to tell."

"What do you mean by that?" the young Chinese asked, before Mei-lang could check him.

"I mean you would have run into gunfire just as Greenwood did. When you found the mine there was no one there. Your problem has changed drastically since you returned to town, William. It's no longer just a case of whether Henry Greenwood's daughter can lay claim to the Lost Buckaroo or if you and your associates in Lum Duck's company can nail it down for your own; you know now that there's a third angle to be considered, and a dangerous one, at that. Other men have their eyes on the mine and they've proven they're ready to kill to get it."

Rip turned to Seng Mei-lang.

"I can't say how rich the Lost Buckaroo is. Apparently a great fortune hangs in the balance. I am sure that is why you are here—to protect the rights of your people to it." He shook his head regretfully. "You have known for a long time that I would stop at nothing in your behalf. There's always been absolute frankness between us in the past— I can't understand all this evasion. Is it possible you have had to bow to the will of these men? I mean

Quan Chew and Lum Duck."

Mei-lang's lips parted in an amused smile.

"Suppose we permit them to answer for themselves," said she. "You, Duck Lum—what have you to say?"

The old man scowled darkly and did not answer. Quan Chew spoke to him in Chinese. It drew an immediate reply, and for several minutes they harangued each other, their violent gutturals harsh and angry.

The partners did not understand a word of it, but they realized there was a difference of opinion between the two elderly men. They saw William silently appeal to Seng Mei-lang to put an end to the bickering. She shook her head resolutely, insisting that they reach a decision.

Finally Lum Duck capitulated. Mei-lang put a question to him and he nodded his agreement.

"That's the way it should have been from the first, Mr. Ripley," said William. "That's how Miss Seng, my father, and I wanted it. Lum Duck was opposed to our saying anything about the Lost Buckaroo."

Rainbow waited for Mei-lang to speak.

"I know you and Grumpy will forgive us for foolishly trying to make you believe we knew nothing about the mine," she said. "It was only because I was convinced you would realize at once that we weren't giving you the whole truth that I gave in to Duck Lum. As he has just said, the promise of great wealth warped his mind. William found the Lost Buckaroo, of course. If you want to ask him anything further about it, he's free to answer."

"There'll be time for that later," Rip told her. "The important thing now is to decide on what we're going to do tomorrow. Grumpy and I will see the sheriff and D.A. early in the morning. You be at the courthouse by nine o'clock, William, and have Doctor Soong with you. I hope we can get McCaffery to string along with us. A lot is going to depend on whether he does or not."

"Are William and the doctor likely to be put under arrest?" Mei-lang asked.

"I hope not. We can't even afford to have William held for questioning. By tomorrow evening, we want to be heading for the Solomons, or we'll be too late. We couldn't hold the news back if we tried; it would be sure to leak out. I prefer to have it break with a bang and see it spread all over the front page of the *Wolf River Gazette*. We'll help our cause by letting it be known that Lum Duck is hurriedly outfitting a party of prospectors for the Solomons and the two of us are going along with them. That should get us some action."

"It shore will!" Grumpy declared, grasping what Rip had in mind. "It'll smoke out the rats that got the professor and start them to makin' tracks for the mine! It'll be a race to see who gits there first!"

"Do you really mean to make the long trip, or is this just a trick to force their hands?" William inquired. "We can travel faster with the carts than they can with burros."

"No bluff about it, William; we'll go—either with you or without you; we can't wait. We'll need half a dozen men in all. They want to be men who can stand up to gunfire. We'll have to depend on you to pick three. Our play would be airtight if we could only produce some evidence that Henry Greenwood had found the Lost Buckaroo. An ore sample that Perce Robbins would be willing to say was identical with those Johnnie Bidwell left with him would do it."

"I took some samples, when I was at the mine," young Chew informed him. "You can use them—if you think the deception is justifiable."

"Perfect!" Rainbow exclaimed. "If deception will help us to round up these killers, I'll take full responsibility for it. You give me the samples tonight; I'll hand them to the D.A., and he can pass them on to Robbins."

Mei-lang had crossed the room and stood at one of the windows, where a goldfish bowl reposed on a teakwood pedestal. Though the tiny fish, flashing about in the bowl, seemed to hold her complete attention, she had not missed a word.

"Rainbow, won't William and Duck Lum's company be endangering their interest in the mine by establishing the fact that Professor Greenwood found it?" she inquired.

"I don't see how," he replied, after thinking it over. "Legally, the Lost Buckaroo is still in the public domain. It belongs to no one."

"I know," she protested, "but the courts have sometimes held that proof of discovery represents a valid claim even though no monuments were erected nor any recording made."

"We found no monuments," William declared. "If Professor Greenwood put them up, either the flood, or the men who killed him, destroyed them."

"Did you find any evidence that the professor had been there?"

"There was evidence that someone had been there within the past few months, Mr. Ripley. There were acid stains on the main vein that were undoubtedly made by a man with scientific knowledge. I don't doubt for a moment that it was Professor Greenwood."

The conversation had taken a turn that was painful to Quan Chew and even more so to Lum Duck. Though old Lum liked to make white men believe that he found their language as difficult to understand as to speak, he missed very little that was said in his hearing. Quan Chew and he had discussed their right, title, and interest in the Lost Buckaroo with Seng Mei-lang at tiresome length. He wasn't any sentimentalist; he admitted that William might not have found the mine but for Henry Greenwood. It was not his idea, however, that once his company had taken possession of the property and fought off all attempts to take it away from them that they should share the prize with the professor's daughter and heir. He had been overruled; even Quan Chew had sided against him.

Lum knew what was coming now and he winced when Rip said, "Let's be honest about this; morally, if not legally, Miss Greenwood has first claim on the mine. If, and when, we can get a conviction against the men who killed her father and Moy Kim, it will eliminate them, no matter if they have registered the property in the meantime and done the assessment work. In the end, if there's a contest, it will be between your people and Lane Greenwood. I know you've talked this over, Mei-lang. How do you feel about it?"

"We want to be generous with Miss Greenwood. William has insisted on that from the first, and I agree with him fully. If she will recognize our rights, we will recognize hers. But we don't intend to be dealt out, to use one of your good American expressions."

"That sounds fair to me," the tall man replied. "I can't speak for Lane Greenwood, but I believe she'll be disposed to be just as generous with you. I know she will feel deeply obligated to William for finding her father."

"There's jest one fly in the ointment," Grumpy observed.

"You mean Del Blanchard?" William was quick to ask.

"Yeh," the little man acknowledged. "He's a young minin' engineer like you. He's goin' to marry Lane. It's only natural that he'd see a great opportunity for himself in developin' the mine from scratch. He may go all out to persuade her not to play ball with you. Course, that's lookin' a long way ahead; we ain't got hold of the Lost Buckaroo yet."

"It's not looking too far ahead," said Rip. "It's something that can be settled easier now than later. Everything considered, I think the Lost Buckaroo should be developed and operated by you and your company, William. I'm sure that's how Henry Greenwood would want it. I believe I can make Lane see it that way, and Del, too. I suppose it'll be up to me to break the news to her that her father's body has been recovered. I'll have to do it tonight; I want her to know what we plan to do before I speak to McCaffery and Logan. She'll want to have her father laid to rest in Reno. Del will have to go with her. Before they leave, I want you and William to have a talk with them, Mei-lang, and get things straightened out. You can see them at the hotel, or we'll bring them down."

"If they'll come, I would prefer to meet them here. William has told me enough about Miss Greenwood to fill me with sympathy. I'm glad she has her young man to comfort her."

Young Chew caught Grumpy glancing at his watch. He took the hint and excused himself to get the ore samples.

"I suppose we can expect a great deal of coming and going tomorrow morning," said Mei-lang.

"Only downstairs and in the cellar," Rainbow told her. "It can't be helped. The coroner will give his permission to have the bodies removed. It won't be necessary for you to see anyone."

"It doesn't matter," she murmured. "I'm still thinking about Miss Greenwood. You'll have to tell her, of course, that her father was shot. The undertaker will be still another who will know. I mention it only because I gathered from what you said a few minutes ago that you hoped to get the district attorney to give out a statement to the effect that Professor Greenwood and Moy Kim were drowned."

"That is my intention," Rainbow agreed. "I know Miss Greenwood can be trusted. As far as Wolf River is concerned, if the hoax holds water for eight to ten hours, I'll be satisfied. If McCaffery gives the word, the coroner can hold up his findings for a day."

Mei-lang shook her head, unable to follow him.

"It's simple enough," said Rip. "McCaffery is going to get the truth from me and nothing but the truth. All of it. He's ambitious. I think I can convince him that it's to his interest to go along with us. There's just three things I want him to do—give out that drowning was the cause of death, say nothing about William having found the mine, palm off the ore samples as having been found on the professor. If he'll go that far with us, we'll know by tomorrow night who the guilty men are."

Quan Chew put down his long Oriental pipe and clapped his hands. It brought in a servant with tea and almond cakes.

It was getting late. The partners were anxious to leave, but they knew that to go without partaking of this proffered hospitality would be unforgivable in Oriental eyes.

William returned with the samples. Grumpy was more interested in them than Rip. He put on his glasses and examined the rich fragments of rock with great care.

"Beautiful stuff!" he muttered. "Beautiful! Too bad as

good a man as Henry Greenwood had to have his life snuffed out over it. At least he had the satisfaction of knowin' he found it. The dirty skunks that downed him couldn't take that away from him."

"And it wasn't luck, Mr. Gibbs, that led him to the Lost Buckaroo," said William; "just his perseverance and cold science. He was not only a good man; he was a great man."

Rainbow let them talk and turned to Mei-lang. He had hoped to have a moment alone with her but he realized that wasn't possible tonight. His thoughts were close to the surface as he gazed at her. She looked up, and her eyes laid a tender caress on him.

"You haven't mentioned it," said he, "but I know you intend to go with us tomorrow evening."

She laughed.

"There's a great understanding in you at times, Rainbow. Have I your permission to accompany you?"

"I said no to Lane Greenwood, but I can't say no to you—not after what we've been through together. It'll be a hard trip and dangerous, too, but I know you'll stand up to it much better than some of us."

"Then, I may go?"

"You can go wherever I go, Mei-lang—"

Suddenly he was not talking about the trip into the desert. She understood him perfectly.

"If only that were possible," she whispered. She shook her head regretfully. "But it isn't, my darling. There are some chains that can't be broken." Her tone changed abruptly. "When you leave here tonight, I'll see that you are well guarded until you are over the hill. I'm afraid some attempt may be made to kill you. Your life is precious to me. Promise you'll be careful."

Rip smiled reassuringly.

"I'll be all right. Instead of giving us an escort, keep your men here and have them guard the cellar. I wouldn't like to see those bodies disappear during the night."

Chapter Eleven

ACCORDING TO PLAN

"I'M AFRAID WHAT YO'RE GOIN' TO SAY to McCaffery and Logan ain't goin' to set so well with them," Grumpy observed as he and Rainbow walked to the courthouse, next morning. "I don't care how you put it, it's goin' to show 'em up. They had this case dumped in their lap months ago and they muffed it completely. They ain't likely to take kindly to the idea of stringin' along with us and playin' second fiddle—leastwise McCaffery won't."

"Go on!" Rip urged. "You've got something on your mind. Let's hear it."

"Wal, he'll be thinkin' of what this is goin' to do to him. You can be shore of that. Instead of goin' up there and tellin' him what we want him to do and why, we can if and but him till he suddenly sees how this business oughta be handled. It'll be yore idea, Rip, but if we can make him think it's his, he'll go for it hook, line, and sinker."

The tall man smiled.

"That's not bad at all," he acknowledged. "We can kick this thing around until there's only one way for him to jump."

They found William and the doctor waiting for them and were relieved to learn that the night had passed without incident in Chinatown.

At Rainbow's suggestion, the two Chinese agreed to wait in an outer office until they were called in.

McCaffery was already at his desk. At Rip's request, he sent down for the sheriff.

Logan walked in a few minutes later and was surprised to find the partners there.

"Looks like there's something doing," he observed lightly. "I noticed Willie Chew and Doc Soong waiting outside. Why did you bring them in, Mac?"

"Ripley and Gibbs brought them; you'll have to ask them why."

"We'll get to that in a minute," said Rainbow. "You better sit down, Shep. We think we may have got to the bottom of the Greenwood matter. It's a long story."

The tall man didn't get far with his statement before the district attorney and Logan lost their boredom. The former began to fidget nervously.

"Is this just talk, or have you got the evidence to back it up?" he burst out.

"That'll have to be for you and Shep to determine," Rip said conciliatingly. "Let me finish; it'll save time."

Long before he was done, the information he laid before them had become so detailed that there was no disputing its authenticity.

Logan's immediate reaction was characteristic.

"So Greenwood actually found the Lost Buckaroo!" he exclaimed. "I suppose it's worth millions!"

McCaffery got to his feet to pace back and forth, appalled by the thought of what these disclosures might do to his political career. Indignation and resentment boiled over in him. Trying to find a goat, he turned on Logan.

"This is a fine kettle of fish you've got us in!" he charged in exasperation. "It was your idea that Greenwood was drowned! I was fool enough to be taken in by it!"

"Mac, you don't have to blow your top like that," Shep protested. "All we had to go on was circumstantial evidence. That can throw anybody. I don't want to take anything away from Rip and Grumpy, but if young Chew and his old man had come to us instead of to them, we'd have known as much as they do."

"Well, they didn't come to us!" McCaffery lashed back. "And they'll pay for it! Soong will lose his license if I can do anything about it! Will you tell me, Ripley, why those Chinks went to you with their story?"

"I told you why; they were afraid. Grump and I have always got along fairly well with the Chinese, thanks to Miss Seng. You haven't any reason to complain; you've got all the cards in your hand now. It's up to you and Logan to round up the men who killed Greenwood and Moy Kim. You wouldn't have had a chance if young Chew had babbled his story as soon as he got back."

"I don't get you!" McCaffery returned.

"I'll try to explain," Rainbow said patiently. "It's our idea that the men you want are in Wolf River. They know the bodies have been recovered, but there's no reason to believe they suspect there's evidence that gunplay figured in the deaths of the two men. And certainly they don't know that William found the mine. If all the facts had been disclosed, you can be sure those birds wouldn't be here now. They're evidently smart enough to realize they're safe for the time being if they just sit tight. I don't know how you're going to smoke them out. We haven't doped out any plan."

"We ought to be able to work out a move," said Shep. "If we can grab 'em, Mac, we'll more than square ourselves."

The district attorney began to recover his poise. He slipped back into his chair and muttered an apology for losing his temper.

"Give me a few minutes—I'll think of something," he promised.

"I couldn't tell you jest how to work it, but I figger the best way to git them to open up is make 'em think they're absolutely in the clear," Grumpy observed. "You don't have to let 'em know the professor and the Chinaman were shot."

"That's an idea," McCaffery acknowledged.

Rainbow pretended to be unimpressed.

"That's all right as far as it goes," he said, "but you can't keep them from finding out that William located the mine. When they learn that the Chinese have the Lost Buckaroo, they won't be fools enough to try to grab it a second time."

The hook was nicely baited, and McCaffery took it with the enthusiasm of a mountain trout.

"I don't know why we can't keep our mouths shut about young Chew finding the mine," he declared rather contemptuous of Rainbow's judgment. "We can do a lot if we have to. I'm beginning to see how to handle this thing."

He mentioned the coroner and that it would be necessary to view the bodies at once.

"I can get Bunting to hold up his official verdict a day or two," he continued. "All I'll give out is that Chew and his men found the bodies in the sand and brought them in, and that Bunting says it was a case of drowning."

The partners looked wise and said nothing. They saw the sheriff shaking his head, and they were delighted when he asked, "Just how is that going to work out, Mac? If that's going to be your story, then nobody's found the Lost Buckaroo. That ain't going to stir up those gents. You got to make them think they're in danger of losing the mine."

"You're right," Rip agreed. "You've put your finger on it, Shep."

The ore samples William had given Rainbow were on McCaffery's desk. He gazed at them in deep abstraction for some moments.

Rainbow and the little one let him take his time, satisfied that he would pounce on the only logical solution sooner or later.

Presently, a grunt of satisfaction escaped the young district attorney. He looked up from his contemplation of the samples with a knowing grin.

"I've got it!" he announced. "Willie didn't find these samples, you understand? Greenwood did. We found them on him this morning. That ought to do it."

"It shore will!" Grumpy agreed enthusiastically. "You couldn't improve on it, less you got Perce Robbins to look at this stuff. He'd have to say it was the same ore Johnnie Bidwell brought him, years ago. That would nail it down for keeps."

Shep Logan called it a smart idea.

Rainbow gave it his approval. He had succeeded more easily than he had expected. Without stressing the point, he pointed out the importance of letting the public know exactly where the bodies had been found.

"It's a clever scheme you've worked out," he told McCaffery. "I congratulate you for thinking of it; I don't see how it can miss. You can count on us to play right along with you. Just what do you think will happen when the news breaks?"

"Why, I believe we'll get some action within a few hours," the district attorney declared confidently. It was balm to his ego to find the partners deferring to him. "I'll give those rats no reason to believe they're under suspicion. Making public where Greenwood was found and that he had located the Lost Buckaroo before he lost his life will provide them with a valid reason for getting their outfit together and going out to locate the mine. We'll take them into custody before they can get out of town."

"*Jee*rusalem, no!" Grumpy protested. "You've got too pat a hand to play it that way! Arrestin' 'em is one thing, gittin' a conviction is another!"

"I suppose it could be handled your way," Rip declared diplomatically, sensing that the redheaded prosecutor was about to flare up. "But you can't produce any witnesses to the crime. If you grab them now, you'll just about have to depend on wringing a confession out of them. I think you can work up a lot stronger case if you'll hold off for a while."

"The boys are right," the sheriff agreed. "We've got to give those gents more rope, Mac. I think we'll do a lot better if we let them pull out for the Solomons and follow them in a day or two later. I can find them. I'll swear in some men and catch those babies squatting on the mine."

"I can't see it!" McCaffery said flatly. "It won't help us a bit, Shep!"

"Sure it will! They'll resist arrest, and that'll be further proof of their guilt." Logan turned to Rainbow. "What do you think, Rip?"

"I agree with Mac; I'm against your idea for a couple reasons." Rainbow spoke with complete honesty; he didn't propose to have his plans scrambled by such a move as the sheriff was suggesting. "We don't know how many men we're dealing with—two—three, maybe half a dozen. One of them has shown us he's got brains. I figure he'll be cute enough to leave someone behind to tip him off to any move you make. But that's the least of my objections. William Chew and his Chinese located the mine, found the bodies, and have given us what evidence we possess. They're entitled to all the consideration we can show them. I can't see us allowing a bunch of blacklegs to take possession of the Lost Buckaroo on the theory that Mac can convict them of murder and wipe out any claim they have on the mine. I guaranteed William, if he held off, we'd see that he got a square deal. I take it that you know all these Chinese prospectors work together. Old Lum Duck is the head of their organization. They could have filed on the property several days ago and sent a party out to hold the mine until everything was settled."

"There may be something to what you say," Logan admitted grudgingly, "but those Chinamen ain't got no right to the Lost Buckaroo, it belongs to Greenwood's daughter. Ain't that right, Mac?"

"I wouldn't care to say offhand," was the noncommittal answer. "I see Ripley's point." He swung around in his chair and directed a question at Rainbow. "Have you talked things over with Miss Greenwood?"

"Last night. She wants to take her father to Reno for burial. Blanchard will go with her. They'll be gone three or four days. That's if you will give her your permission to take the body."

"I don't object to that," the district attorney declared. "What I was referring to was the mine. Has anything been said about that?"

"Yes. She has expressed her willingness to share it with William and his associates. They're equally willing to enter into such an arrangement. When we finish, Grump and I are going to take Miss Greenwood down to Chinatown for a conference. That end of it doesn't trouble me.

The big question is, how you are going to proceed."

"I'm going to look before I leap. I can't afford to make a mistake, Ripley. I know I haven't got the right answer yet."

"I reckon yo're closer to it than you figger," Grumpy volunteered. "The Chinks are in this up to their necks. Why don't you use 'em?"

"How?"

"Why, ain't it goin' to look mighty queer if they let another bunch of men pull away from town without doin' somethin' about it? Lord knows they got the inside track on the mine. I figger they'd be the first ones to light out for the Solomons."

"That's right!" McCaffery agreed. "Go on!"

"Wal, you've got the authority, Mac, to call the tune. Here's young Willie and Doc Soong waitin' outside, shakin' in their boots for fear yo're goin' to clamp down on 'em for not reporting to you at once. If you read the riot act to 'em for a few minutes and then tell Willie yo're willin' to forgit everythin' if he'll play ball with you, he'll fall over himself to take you up. If you say he's to be ready to pull out by evenin', with a bunch of friends, they'll be ready. As an afterthought, you can tell him Rip and I'll go with them. We'll git to the mine first. When those other gents show up, we'll hold 'em off. That'll set things up for Shep to walk in with his deputies."

Logan slapped his knee.

"That's it, Mac! It's perfect!"

The district attorney pursed his lips thoughtfully. Though he failed to give Grumpy's suggestion his approval, he liked the idea and wished he had thought of it himself.

"How does it strike you, Ripley?" he inquired cagily.

"It sounds all right to me. We'd have to make sure of our timing. There's bound to be some gunsmoke in this business. We wouldn't want to find ourselves looking for Shep and his deputies and not see them showing up."

"We'd be there whenever you said," Logan assured him. "How much time would you want me to give you?"

"Three days would be about right. If we go through with this, we'll pull out this evening. You should shove off Saturday night, or no later than Sunday morning. But what's the sense of getting down to brass tacks till we know Mac's decision. It's up to him to say yes or no."

"It's okay with me," McCaffery announced. "You all seem to be sold on it. Are you sure, Ripley, that the Chinamen will take orders from you and Gibbs?"

"Absolutely. If you think there's any doubt of that, you can mention to William that Grumpy and I are to be the headmen. But that isn't necessary. If you'll allow us to organize our party as we please and take charge of it without putting any strings on us, I guarantee you the Chinese will hold up their end."

They continued to talk over their plans for another ten minutes, when Rip got to his feet.

"You better get William and the doctor in here," he suggested. "Grump and I will step outside. I'd advise you to see Doctor Soong first, and alone. He'll lose face if you rake him over the coals in front of William. You know what that means to an educated Chinese."

The D.A. nodded.

"Send him in. I won't bear down too hard on him. We'll go down to Chinatown as soon as I get through with them. You get hold of Bunting, Shep. Tell him I want him right away. Don't tell him why."

The partners exchanged a relieved glance. They had

been skating on thin ice for the past few minutes, with all their maneuvering likely to go for naught unless they could post William on what he was to say. The opportunity was theirs now, and after Logan hurried off to find the coroner, and Doctor Soong had gone in to talk to the district attorney, they sat down with young Chew.

"You were in there a long time," said William. He did not attempt to conceal his anxiety.

"It's going to work out all right," Rip told him. "But get this straight, William, when Mr. McCaffery tells you what we're going to do, don't you give him any reason to think you heard any part of it from us last night. He believes the action we're going to take is his idea. Don't you say anything to the contrary. Understand?"

William smiled obliquely.

"I think I do. You are very clever, gentlemen. As my honorable father so often says, 'If one finds an obstacle in his path, it serves just as well to go around it as over it.' "

When the partners were convinced that Chew understood what was expected of him, they went downstairs. The little one was jubilant.

"By grab, there's more'n one way to skin a cat!" he declared. "All we had to do was to let McCaffery think he was callin' the shots."

"It's a good thing we did," said Rip. "He'd have jumped over the traces if we'd gone about it any other way."

They were standing at the head of the courthouse steps, when Logan returned with a dried-up little man who proved to be Eli Bunting, the coroner.

After exchanging a word or two with the partners, Bunting and the sheriff continued on up to McCaffery's office.

Rainbow ran an eye over the little town. Wolf River dozed peacefully in the brilliant morning sunshine. There wasn't a cloud in the sky. A man was sluicing down the sidewalk in front of the Silver Dollar. It was Pat McGarry. Every time he came out with a bucketful of water, he managed a glance at the courthouse.

Just inside the swinging doors of the saloon, Blanton and Cleve Miller waited for the reports he brought them.

"Logan and Buntin' jest went up," Pat came in to tell them. "No sign of the two Chinks yet. Reckon they're still chewin' the fat with McCaffery."

"Where's Ripley and his partner?" Blanton asked.

"Still waitin' by the courthouse door. Ripley was lookin' this way a minute ago."

"Don't let on you see them," Blanton snapped. "Get another bucket of water and get out there, and keep your eyes open!"

McGarry filled his bucket and returned to his very convenient labors. It was not long before he hurried in again, his agitation pronounced.

"The whole bunch of 'em jest came out and struck off across the lots! They're headin' for Chinatown, Cord!"

"Course they are!" Blanton retorted. "That's what we expected them to do! So what?"

Pat nervously wiped his mouth with the back of his hand.

"It's gettin' close," he muttered. "They looked like they was goin' to a wake, walkin' along two by two."

"Our wake, if you ask me!" Cleve droned dismally.

"Will the two of you shut up?" Blanton raged. "I tell you we got nothing to be afraid of! If I hear another peep out of you, the lid won't be the only thing that'll be blown off around here today!"

Chapter Twelve

TOO MANY SUSPECTS

FRED BUSBY, THE EDITOR AND PUBLISHER of the *Wolf River Gazette,* could count on the fingers of one hand the times he had rushed out an extra edition of his newspaper. "Rushed" was not to be taken too literally, for the *Gazette* was hand-set. To make up a new front page and put Dennis McCaffery's statement in type took better than an hour. In the meantime, the startling news had been traveling far and wide by word of mouth, and long before the extra edition was off the press, everyone in Wolf River knew the Lost Buckaroo had been found, as well as the other salient points of the story.

Shopkeepers and their customers moved out to the plank sidewalk to catch whatever new details were being handed up and down the street. Business was at a standstill. Even the saloon loafers had stepped out into the sunlight to catch all the currents of information and express their weighty opinions as to what all this excitement meant. In addition to the townspeople, several score of sleepy-eyed miners from the night shift on Midas Mountain, had been caught up by the excitement and stood around in little groups in front of their boardinghouses and favorite haunts.

There was a turning of heads when the partners left the Union House with Lane and Blanchard, bound for Chinatown. Many recognized her and fell silent as she passed.

"Look there! Such a mob tryin' to hear what Robbins has got to say that they can't all git in," Grumpy remarked, as they neared the assayer's office.

Rainbow nodded and said nothing; he saw it was an ordeal for Lane to have to face all these people, believing, with good reason, that among them were the men who had killed her father. He was relieved when they left the main street behind them and neared the Chinese quarter. He had had the professor's remains removed to a local undertaker's establishment, where they were being prepared for shipment that afternoon.

Hoping to make this first meeting of Lane and Mei-lang as brief as possible, that he and Grumpy might be free to watch the developing situation in town, he left them alone together, with William and Del.

On the surface, the excitement of the morning in Chinatown had subsided, and in the few minutes that the partners sat talking with Quan Chew, only a group of curious, gesticulating children watched the building from a vantage point across the way.

A step sounded on the stairs presently. It was William. He announced that an understanding satisfactory to all had been reached.

"There was a difference of opinion between Del and me, but we worked that out," he ran on. "I understand there is great excitement uptown."

"Yes," said Rip. "That's why we're so anxious to get back. Have you picked our men for the expedition?"

"All but one, Mr. Ripley. I want Wah Chang to go with us. He's out at the Kingsley ranch, visiting his brother. He'll be here during the afternoon. Chang's been with me all summer. We couldn't have a better man."

"I want every man to go armed. I mean with a high-powered rifle."

"I've arranged for that," the young Chinese informed him. "We'll take food enough to last us three weeks. Water won't be a problem. Is there anything else, Mr. Ripley?"

"Just be sure you have everything ready, so we can pull out on a few minutes' notice. And you better arrange to keep in touch with us during the afternoon. If you don't find us at the hotel, try the courthouse."

Mei-lang came down with Lane and Blanchard. Lane spoke of Moy Kim with deep affection.

"Kim was a good man," she said. "He was with us so long that we regarded him as one of the family. I'm so happy to know he's to have a ceremonial service. I want to pay the expenses for the mourners and the funeral feast."

"We can talk about that later, when you return to Wolf River," Mei-lang told her. Turning to Rip, she asked if anyone had come under his suspicion since the district attorney had spoken.

"No, it's a little early for that," he replied. "But I'm sure something will break shortly."

Grumpy and he went to the train with Lane and Del. It lacked a few minutes of three, when they got back to the hotel. They found a small crowd gathered on the plank sidewalk in front of the Union House. Tom Stewart, the rotund mayor of the town, was in the center of it and taking some good-natured ribbing from his friends.

"Yo're the plumpest desert rat I ever laid eyes on!" one of them called out. "Wait till the sun gits to work on that tallow yo're packin' around! You'll melt away to a shadder, Tom!"

Stewart joined in the laugh at his expense.

"Don't you worry about me, Clem," he retorted. "I'll keep right up with the lads I'm going in with, soon as I get my second wind. That desert country don't scare me even a little bit."

The partners' eyes met in quick understanding. It wasn't necessary to ask. Tom Stewart was going after the Lost Buckaroo!

He discussed his plans so freely that Rip and the little one had only to listen to learn that two Wolf River men were to go with him. One of them, Bucky Smith, had done some prospecting but spent most of his time tending bar. The other, Dave Trammell, though never a desert rat, had apparently been associated with mining in some capacity for most of his life, and always with indifferent success. "Hard-luck Dave" the partners heard him called.

"You'll be lucky to come out alive, if you depend on them two fellas to tell you where you are," one of Stewart's friends advised.

"I don't aim to depend on them," Tom returned. "I wanted Wild Bill to go in with us, but Blanton beat me to it. Bill's goin' with him. But I got Dad Ritchie comin' down from Battle Mountain on the evenin' train. Dad knows that country as well as Wild Bill."

"You won't be alone down there," the hotel barber told Stewart. "It ain't only Cord Blanton's bunch that'll be keepin' you company; some boys from the Midas are throwin' up their jobs and lightin' out for the Solomons, too."

"That's all okay with me," Tom declared. "We got as good a chance as anybody."

Rip caught the little one's eye and they drew aside. They had not counted on the news starting such a stampede as this.

"Take it easy," Rip advised, sensing that Grumpy was ready to explode. "We set up this game, and we've got to stick with it, no matter what happens."

"But Stewart!" Grumpy jerked out incredulously. "He was the last man I figgered might be mixed up in this business! And Blanton goin' after the mine, too! And another bunch from Midas! I don't know what to think!"

"You get in there and draw Stewart out. I'd like to know how he got this Dad Ritchie, from Battle Mountain, lined up so quickly. Don't make any crack about our plans. We'll try that on him a little later."

Grumpy was a past master at injecting himself into a conversation and getting out of it what he wanted. He edged back into the crowd and eased himself into the discussion. It wasn't long before he was buttonholing Stewart.

"I don't know what's so peculiar about my bein' interested in a gold mine," the latter protested in response to a query from the little one. "I been takin' flyers all my life."

"You musta been thinkin' about it for some time," Grumpy averred. "I reckon McCaffery no more'n opened his mouth than you was ready to jump the gun—goin' after Wild Bill and gittin' hold of this party in Battle Mountain."

"By gum, it don't take me all week to make up my mind, when I want to do somethin'! I wasn't quick enough on the draw to git Wild Bill, but I didn't lose no time telegraphin' Dad Ritchie!"

"And you got him, eh?"

"Sure! He answered pronto."

With cunning indirection, Grumpy learned that Stewart planned to leave Wolf River as soon as his man arrived from the north. To speed things up, he was going to load his burros and gear in a wagon and drive to the Jensen ranch on Calamity Creek.

"We'll be shovin' off from there tomorrow mornin', come daylight," Tom told him.

Beyond that, he refused to go, other than to say that he had a trick or two up his sleeve.

"We know what we're after and we think we know where to find it and how to git there first," he said. His tone and manner had changed suddenly and he was no longer the good-natured, bantering fat man. "I ain't tippin' nobody off to how we're goin' to play our hand. If there's trouble—and I mean gun trouble—we'll be ready for it."

"Was that meant for me, Tom?"

The query came from the edge of the crowd, and it was thin and definitely unfriendly.

The partners knew, without turning, that Cord Blanton had voiced it. He had evidently come up just in time to catch Stewart's warning.

"You can suit yourself about that," the mayor retorted. "If we git our hands on the mine, it's goin' to take somethin' more than a bluff to pry us loose. That goes for you as well as for anyone else."

Blanton laughed quietly.

"That goes two ways," said he. "You didn't expect to have the field to yourself, did you?"

"No, it's a free-for-all. But it ain't goin' to be healthy for anybody who tries to crowd us."

Cord laughed again, and his laughter had a mocking note.

"You won't see us for dust, Tom! If you're sore because

I grabbed Wild Bill ahead of you, forget it. I been in that country. There's a thousand canyons, running every which way. If we don't find the Lost Buckaroo, we'll at least have a look at the strike my partners made down there this spring. We're going in six strong, and we don't intend to ask permission of anyone about where we want to head for."

"That's all right—as far as it goes—but don't step on our toes, Blanton; that's all I got to tell you."

Tom elbowed his way through the crowd and up the steps into the hotel.

"Blanton, you and Stewart sound right hostile," Grumpy observed thinly. "Must be the two of you realize yo're goin' out to pick a dead man's pocket."

Cord pulled down the corners of his mouth and regarded the little one unfavorably.

"I don't know about that," he declared contemptuously. "My conscience don't bother me. If it's your idea that because Greenwood found the mine it belongs to his daughter, you got another guess coming. I ain't waiting around for some other party to grab it."

Rip said nothing. He was satisfied that the little man could hold his own with Blanton.

"Be quite a blow to all you gents, who are hot-footin' it into the Solomons, if the courts said it was hers," Grumpy declared.

"I'll take a chance on that," Blanton snapped. "Possession is nine points of the law." He turned to Rainbow. "What about your Chinese friends, Ripley? Don't tell me they're dealing themselves out of the Lost Buckaroo."

"I don't believe they are," Rip said lightly. "If you're really curious, why don't you ask them?"

"I have," Cord admitted bluntly. "I stopped young

Willie down the street a few minutes ago. He closed up like a clam. But that don't fool me. Those yellow boys are going after it, all right. And I don't mind telling you I'm a lot more worried about them beating us to it than Tom Stewart or this other bunch from the Midas."

"My Chinese friends—as you put it—will look out for themselves, I imagine. At least, they know where to begin looking for the Lost Buckaroo."

The tall man was deliberately needling Blanton. He had changed his mind, however, about saying anything in regard to his own plans, feeling that the need for it was gone. Having given Cord opportunity to commit himself, he waited for him to do something about it.

"It gives them an edge," was Blanton's candid—and artful—admission. He wasn't to be tripped by such a simple ruse.

Rip asked him about the miners from the Midas. Blanton dismissed them contemptuously.

"They don't mean a thing, Ripley. A big gorilla by the name of Ike Nelson is the head of the outfit. You acquainted with him?"

The tall man said no.

"Nelson's got three of his sidekicks tagging along with him. They're a tough bunch; they're in my place every day, shooting the breeze. Maybe they know something about mining, but they don't know from nothing when it comes to desert prospecting. If they don't give it up for a bad job before they get through Toquima Basin, I'll be surprised."

"They wouldn't be blowin' their money on an outfit if they didn't figger they had a chance," a bystander commented. "You better not count 'em out yet, Cord."

Blanton grinned.

"Maybe you're right, Ed. I got something to do besides standing here gabbing."

He turned to make his way through the crowd, when Rip asked, "I don't suppose you're saying anything about how soon you'll be pulling out?"

"No secret about that," Cord answered lightly. "We'll be on our way in an hour or two."

Chapter Thirteen

RACE FOR GOLD—AND GUILT

WITH BLANTON'S DEPARTURE, the crowd dissolved.

"Come on, Grump," Rainbow muttered. "We better get hold of McCaffery before he comes looking for us. With things shaping up this way, he may walk out on us."

"That's what I'm afraid of," the little one growled as he fell into step with him. "We certainly didn't make any hay with Stewart or Blanton. This fella Nelson may be our man. You goin' to try to say anythin' to him?"

"No, we'll let the chips ride as they are. We know there's three parties setting out. There may be more. That'll put the heat on the men we want; they'll make a beeline for the mine. That'll be the tip-off."

"No two ways about that," the little one agreed. "They won't stall around, tryin' to make us think they don't know where to find what they're lookin' for. Neither Stewart nor Blanton seemed at all curious about what we're goin' to do. You figger they know?"

"I doubt it," said Rip. "But you can be sure we're not being counted out of this by the men who killed Greenwood. We'll make this short and sweet with McCaffery. If Logan's up there with him, so much the better."

They found the sheriff and district attorney together. They saw at a glance that the latter was in a dither.

"What have the three of you let me in for?" he demanded furiously. "I didn't hear any of you say this morning that this thing could kick back and slap me in the face!"

He was well informed as to what had happened. Rainbow let him blow off steam without interruption. When McCaffery finished, the tall man told him he and Grumpy had just talked with Stewart and Blanton. He repeated what they had had to say.

"That doesn't get us anywhere!" McCaffery fumed. "If I—"

"Just a minute, Mac," Rip cut him off. "Suppose you listen to me for once. We agreed with Shep that this business wasn't going to be played out short of the Solomons. That still goes. We didn't figure on all this excitement. But it's even better than what we expected. I don't care if half the town sets out to find the Lost Buckaroo. It wouldn't change the fact that only the men who killed Henry Greenwood and Moy Kim know where the mine is located. As I told Grumpy, they'll make a beeline for it now. That's just what we want them to do. It'll come mighty close to being evidence enough in itself to convict them."

"That's what I been trying to tell you, Mac!" Logan burst out. "I didn't see it quite your way, Rip, but it's just horse sense that the gents who win the race will be our meat. You can't figure otherwise."

McCaffery was hard to convince.

"I suppose I've got to string along with you," he admitted reluctantly. "I'm in so deep now I can't pull out. When are you fellows going to get away?"

"We'll let the others pull out before we do anything," Rainbow told him. "William says he hasn't been going through the basin lately. By keeping to the west, it saves ten miles or more, he claims. That'll give us quite an edge. We'll travel all night."

"Take a couple blankets apiece," Logan advised. "Gets

mighty cold on that high desert just before dawn. You got everything you need?"

"We'll have to pick up a couple boxes of cartridges for our rifles. We've got binoculars and everything else. It might be better, Shep, if you gave us a day more than we figured on this morning. You leave Wolf River Sunday evening. I'll have William draw a map for you and give you instructions, so you'll know just where to find us. I'll put everything in an envelope and leave it with his father. You can pick it up tomorrow. If we're all set, we'll say so long and get back to the hotel and pack up our junk."

"Okay, Ripley," McCaffery said. "I wish you and Grumpy the best of luck. Lord knows I'll be pulling for you." ·

He got up and shook hands with the partners. Logan did likewise.

"Between us, we'll pull this out of the fire," he declared confidently. "So long!"

The partners were standing at the hotel desk, paying their bill less than an hour later when a man stuck his head in the door and said, "Here comes Nelson's bunch!"

There was a general movement toward the porch by everyone in the lobby. Rip and Grumpy followed the others.

Down the street came four men and two burros. The good-natured chaff flung at the four men drew no response from them. They were a grim, hard-faced crew. Nelson, a brawny, towering giant, swung along at the head of the little procession, a scornful glint in his narrowed eyes. From the packs on the burros, the muzzles of four rifles protruded. They struck an ominous note.

"They're well-heeled, even if they are travelin' light," Grumpy muttered, as the cavalcade passed.

"I noticed," was Rip's only comment.

It was the beginning of the exodus from Wolf River. Nelson's party had no more than disappeared around the shoulder of Midas Mountain, when Blanton and his men strode down the street, with Wild Bill Melody, looking like a scrawny old eagle with his hooked nose and long neck, stepping along at Cord's side. Cleve Miller and Pat McGarry followed, and behind the burros came Buckout and Kumler, the two men Cord had recruited from the Midas.

Wild Bill had supplied the burros, four in number. They were heavily laden. If there were rifles in the packs, they were not visible.

The onlookers gave the party the same reception Nelson had received, with some special attention for Wild Bill. The old man and Blanton took the bantering in their stride, exchanging quip for quip and calling out farewells to acquaintances along the way.

With their passing, the crowd waited, expecting Stewart's party to put in an appearance. The evening train had been in for some minutes.

"I didn't figger Tom would be the last dog hung," the partners overheard a man observe. "Wonder what's holdin' him up?"

"Don't worry 'bout Tom Stewart," the man at his side answered. "He's hired Chris to drive his bunch as far as Jensen's. He'll git there hours ahead of Nelson and Blanton. This is them comin' now!"

A heavy wagon hove into view from the direction of the depot. Stewart sat on the seat with the driver. Standing in the box were Bucky Smith and Trammell and two burros. The mayor held up his hand in a salute to the crowd and urged Chris to whip up his team. In a few minutes, they had left Wolf River behind them.

The partners stepped back into the hotel and went through to the rear entrance, where they found a Chinese waiting with a cart for their gear. They brought it out and saw him wheel it away.

The dining-room was open now.

"We better put away a steak, or somethin' that'll stick with us a few hours," Grumpy advised. "It's just six; we got time."

"Let's go in," Rainbow said. "We've paid for our supper, we might as well eat it."

They were in Chinatown half an hour later, to find that William had completed all arrangements for their departure. The three men he had selected to accompany them were, with the exception of Wah Chang, young, sturdy-looking fellows.

At Rainbow's request, William sat down at his father's desk and penciled the map and instructions for Logan. Mei-lang came down as they sat there. She wore boots, riding-breeches, and woolen shirt, attire well-suited for the long trek. The tall man gave her an approving glance.

"We'll be through here in a minute," he told her. "We're leaving some directions for the sheriff, so he'll be sure to find us."

"Do he and Mr. McCaffery know I'm accompanying you?" she asked.

"No, I said nothing to them. They would have been sure to object. And with good reason."

Mei-lang frowned.

"You don't sound enthusiastic about my going."

"Frankly, I'm not," Rip confessed. "I've seen enough in the last hour to convince me that we're going to have a rougher time than I thought. If I had any reason to think

I could persuade you to remain here, I'd make the effort."

"I'm not making this trip for the thrill of it," she said, with quiet determination. "You may find you need me, Rainbow."

"No doubt," he agreed. "I know I can count on William. The others will not take orders from me the way they will from you."

"I'm looking much farther ahead than that," said Mei-lang. "If we meet with success, I want to be a witness to it; I want to see everything with my own eyes so that in the days to come I can be sure we'll honor to the letter the promises we made Miss Greenwood." Banteringly, she added, "You know, Rainbow, we Chinese aren't above being greedy at times."

Quan Chew overheard the remark. Chuckling over it, he spread his fat hands in a deprecatory gesture.

"Not this time, Mr. Ripley," he protested. "We squabble over the crumbs but not over the whole loaf."

With only a little group of the curious to see them off, they left the quarter. By following the wash for several miles, they avoided passing through Wolf River. Turning south, they had a wide, sagebrush-covered plain ahead of them.

Night fell before they were halfway across. Before long, the stars came out to light their way. Wah Chang roamed far ahead, trying to find easy going for the carts. Mei-lang swung along between the partners, exchanging only an occasional word with them.

The moon came up finally, shedding its soft effulgence over the desert. Far ahead, low hills loomed. Rip called William's attention to them.

"We'll be able to avoid them," the young Chinese assured him. "Just beyond them, we'll drop down into

Spirit Valley. It'll take us three to four hours to get through it."

Shortly after midnight, they called a halt and rested briefly amid surroundings that were ghostly by moonlight. Wind erosion had been at work for centuries in Spirit Valley, carving the soft sandstone dikes and cliffs into fantastic monuments and parapets. From where he sat, smoking his pipe, Grumpy glanced back at the crumbling arch through which they had just pushed the carts.

"Looks to me like that thing's about ready to let go," he observed soberly. "I don't want to be under there when it does."

"It's beautiful, Grumpy," Mei-lang protested.

"It's right purty," the little man admitted, "but I'll walk around it next time."

They pushed on, leaving the valley behind them, and struck across open country that was crisscrossed by shallow arroyos. When the latter could not be avoided, the sharp banks had to be cut down with shovels, and then all hands were required to push the carts across.

Rainbow watched Mei-lang carefully as the night wore on. When he suggested that they stop, she wouldn't have it. An hour before dawn, however, he saw unmistakable signs of weariness in her.

"We've come far enough for tonight," he told William. "We'll sleep for a couple hours."

"You're not doing this on my account, Rainbow?" Mei-lang asked.

"No," he answered. "There's no point in overdoing it; we've got a long, hard day ahead of us tomorrow."

He told William to caution the men against striking a light.

"We're all tired," he said. "If we turn in without showing a light, we won't have to set a guard."

The sense of this was apparent to all. The Chinese crawled under the carts with their blankets and were soon asleep. Rip and Grumpy arranged a tarp to give Mei-lang some privacy. Saying good night, they turned in, too.

The sun was above the horizon when Rainbow sat up in his blankets and surveyed the world about him. A sand hill, a few yards to the south of camp was the only near-by elevation. He pulled on his boots and, taking his binoculars, climbed it at once. Though the hill was not more than seventy feet high, he was able to scan the country in every direction for some distance.

He studied it for minutes and was about to lower the glasses, convinced that in the vast expanse of desert nothing moved, when several specks, far to the east, caught his attention.

"Men and burros!" he muttered tensely.

Though he trained the glasses on them carefully, they were too distant to be recognized. He tried counting them but they seemed to be milling around and he couldn't arrive at the same total twice.

Down below, Wah Chang had a fire going and was boiling water for tea. Rip came down from the hill with a rush and kicked the fire out. The teakettle went bounding away, its clatter arousing everyone and throwing the camp into wide-eyed excitement. Grumpy saw the binoculars in Rip's hand and divined the explanation at once.

"We ain't alone, eh?" he demanded.

"Bunch of men over to the east of us, Grump. I couldn't make out who they are. They must have come through without stopping to get this far. As near as I can make out, they're going to bed now."

He turned to William.

"I don't want any smoke drifting across to them. We'll go on for a couple miles before we cook breakfast. You tell Seng Mei-lang there's no reason to be alarmed. We can take our time, pulling away from here."

Mei-lang joined the partners several minutes later. She had slept soundly and looked refreshed. She found them speculating on the identity of the party that had caught up with them. William joined in the conversation.

"It can't be Mr. Stewart," said he. "He was going in by way of the Jensen ranch and the basin."

"I reckon it's Blanton's bunch," Grumpy asserted. "They got this Wild Bill with 'em. He must know all the short cuts."

Mei-lang looked to Rip for his opinion.

"My guess is that it's Blanton," he told them. "It doesn't matter particularly. The important thing is that someone's overhauled us. If we can get away unnoticed, we can pick up several hours on them now. If we keep on moving all day, William, where will we be when night falls?"

"We should be skirting the lower edge of Toquima Basin, Mr. Ripley, at a place called Picture Rocks. They're a curving series of overhanging sandstone cliffs. If we camp there tonight, we should reach Spanish Tanks by tomorrow evening."

They veered off to the west for some distance before heading south again. During the long day they saw no one. Evening was upon them before they reached Picture Rocks. The wind had been rising during the afternoon and promised to blow all night.

"If she really gits to howlin', we're goin' to eat some sand," the little one complained. The long trek was wearing harder on him than on anyone else in the company. He eyed the cliffs contemplatively. "If we move in, mebbe we can find a pocket and git outa this wind."

Rainbow shook his head.

"We'll be safer out here."

"What do you mean, safer? We ain't seen no one since daylight!"

"That's what makes me spooky," said Rip. "We'll camp out in the sage. That bunch may be using glasses, too."

Before permitting a tiny fire to be built, he called for shovels and had an embankment built around it. Twilight was gone by the time supper was over. The fire was extinguished, and everyone turned in for the night. Sleep came quickly.

Barely an hour later, however, Rip shook Grumpy awake.

"Wake up, Grump!" he rapped. "Somebody's set the sage afire to the west of us! The flames are racing this way!"

Everyone was quickly aroused.

"We'll have to move, Mr. Ripley!" young William cried. "There's just bare sand near the base of the cliffs! We'll be safe there!"

"We're not going in," the tall man said flatly. "The purpose of this fire is to pin us up against the cliffs. We'll stay where we are. Start pulling up sage! As soon as we've got a little space cleared, we'll light some backfires!"

The issue was not in doubt for long; the dry, oily sagebrush broke into flame as soon as it was ignited and began to burn away from camp in all directions leaving nothing for the advancing fire from the west to feed on.

Two of the Chinese, Bow Chee and Gar Lee, suffered

insignificant burns on their hands. There were no other injuries; but the clouds of pungent white smoke that billowed over the camp punished everyone.

"The dirty skunks musta been playin' tag with us all day!" Grumpy growled, between fits of coughing. "Reckon they're up there on the cliffs, enjoyin' theirselves!"

What more he might have said was cut short by a blast of gunfire from the rimrock. Scattered shots followed. They were so wide of the mark that Rainbow concluded it was intentional.

"Start throwing lead at them, Grumpy!" he ordered. "That goes for you and your boys, William! Shoot at the gun flashes! If we can stir them up enough, they'll stop this sniping!"

The little one needed no second invitation. He had his gun bucking before Rip finished speaking.

Between shots, Rainbow watched the Chinese and was pleased to see the businesslike way in which they worked their rifles.

The gunfire from the rim continued for a few minutes. When it stopped, it stopped abruptly, and the night was suddenly still again.

"Smoked 'em out of that, I reckon!" Grumpy growled. "What was the idea of all this, anyhow? Seems like they coulda picked some of us off!"

"I'm surprised that you have to ask," Rip returned sharply. "It's plain enough that setting the sage ablaze and banging away with their guns was just a game to discourage us."

The tall man's eyes went to Mei-lang, his anxiety for her unmistakable.

"It was noisy while it lasted," he said. "Were you frightened?"

"No," she murmured, giving him a brave smile. "I'm never afraid when I'm with you."

"I hope you'll be able to say that three or four days from now," Rip returned, trying not to sound too alarming. "This was only a taste of what we can expect. Those fellows were only fooling tonight."

Chapter Fourteen

MESSAGE ON THE DESERT FLOOR

RAINBOW, GRUMPY, AND WILLIAM took turns standing guard, but the rest of the night passed without incident. Everyone was awake shortly after dawn. Mei-lang suggested that they forego breakfast and be on their way at once.

The tall man said no. William and Wah Chang had described Spanish Tanks and the canyon in which the mine was located, with such detail that he had a clear picture of them in his mind. As a result, he was convinced that the Tanks, with their unfailing water supply, were the key to the whole situation. He endeavored to explain this to Mei-lang.

"I don't believe we could overtake the bunch that fired on us last night, no matter how we hurried. I'm satisfied to let them stay ahead of us. They won't go any farther than the Tanks tonight. If the lay of the land is such as William and Chang describe it to be, those fellows will fort up there and have little trouble holding us off. Before morning, they'll slip away and head for the mine."

William's face fell on hearing this. He had been an interested listener.

"But, Mr. Ripley, we don't have to go to Spanish Tanks!" he protested. "We have water enough to last us a week. We can stay west of the Tanks and go up the canyon tonight."

Rainbow shook his head.

"It would be a mistake to get to the mine ahead of them. I thought it out very carefully last night, while I was standing my trick."

This was such a complete reversal of his previous position that it brought Grumpy into the conversation with an acrimonious snort.

"That ain't the way you talked it over with me; and it ain't what you held out to McCaffery and Logan!"

"That's true," Rip acknowledged. "I'll trade a deuce for an ace anytime. You heard what William and Chang had to say about the position of the mine. They place it on a blank, unbroken wall, at the mercy of anyone on the rim, across the canyon. Without any place to hole in, I don't believe we could defend it. No one else is going to stay there long, if they're attacked."

"Grantin' all that, where does it leave us? You talk about pickin' up an ace. Where is it?"

"Spanish Tanks. If we play it right, we can't miss. The first thing to do is to find out who's ahead of us. We'll stay well behind them all day. This evening, after dark, we'll split up. You'll take William, Grump, and work in toward the Tanks. Don't try to go all the way in. You'll be over your head if you do; just lay out in the sand and pump a few shots into them. Play it up enough to give them the idea that they've got all of us out there. I figure you'll be able to walk into the Tanks unmolested, anytime after dawn. Once we get hold of the springs, we'll hang onto them, no matter how anything else goes; nobody can stay in this country very long without water."

"Yo're beginnin' to make sense now," the little one grumbled. "While all this is goin' on, what are you goin' to be doin'?"

"We'll be in the canyon. We won't go as far as the

mine; we'll hide out in the first likely place we find.
Chang will go with us to show the way. I want to be in a
position to see that bunch go directly to the mine. That'll
prove they had previous knowledge of it. It'll give Mc-
Caffery a shut and closed case against them."

Grumpy put his approval on the plan. Young William
didn't like it. Judged by the stream of excited gutturals
that came from his men, they were more opposed to it
than he.

"You better translate what I said," Rip advised Mei-
lang. "I want them to get it straight."

She spoke to them at length, but they continued to pro-
test. William got into the argument, too.

"What seems to be the difficulty?" Rainbow inquired.

"They feel that getting possession of the Lost Buckaroo
should be our first consideration, not building up a case
against the men who killed Professor Greenwood and
Moy Kim."

"But that's the surest way to get hold of the mine,"
Rainbow insisted. "Convict those men and the property
is yours."

"I've explained that to them," said Mei-lang. "I know
you're right." She turned to William suddenly. "Tell
Rainbow what you just told me."

"It's not that I object to your proposal, Mr. Ripley,"
young Chew hastened to say. "I have nothing better to
suggest. What I'm afraid of is, that so much time will
elapse before we win out that the other parties will be
here and we may lose everything in the confusion."

"It won't take that long," Rip said flatly. "What I've
suggested is not only the best line of action we can take,
it's the only one we can hope to get away with. If you or
Chang have any counterproposals, I'm willing to listen

to them. But we're going to thresh this matter out right now."

Mei-lang spoke to William and the others in Chinese again. The partners knew nothing of what she was saying, but they judged from her tone that it was to the point. Grumpy nudged Rainbow.

"She's tellin' 'em, she ain't askin' 'em what we're goin' to do," he muttered under his breath.

Even before she finished, it was apparent that her countrymen had accepted her viewpoint.

"We are agreed that the course you advise is the wise one, Rainbow," she said simply. "There'll be no further misunderstanding about it."

Rip silently thanked her for her intervention. The carts were put in motion, and they continued on their way. The country began to change radically during the course of the day. They left the sagebrush and the occasional clumps of mesquite behind and entered a world that was barren of all vegetation. Far away to the south, the bulk of the Solomon Mountains began to take definite shape.

It was Rip and Grumpy who ranged in advance now, looking for tracks. They cut the trail of the men ahead of them about noon. It told them less than they expected.

"It could be a big party," Grumpy declared. "But you can't be shore; they're strung out in single file and steppin' in one another's tracks."

"They won't travel that way all day," said Rip. "We'll keep after them."

Their patience was not rewarded until they had followed the trail for several miles. To avoid a wide sand drift, the quarry had spread out. The partners studied the message written on the desert floor.

"That's definite!" the little one exclaimed. "Six men

and two burros! That spells Blanton!"

"No question about it," Rainbow agreed. "I don't know as I'm surprised. The facts fall into place too neatly to leave any doubt about who killed Greenwood and Kim. Go back to the beginning, Grump, and you'll see what I mean. When McGarry and Miller hit Wolf River with their story of making a strike, they were faking it. It was done to set up what followed. Blanton pretended to stake them. It gave them a reason for getting into the desert. They tailed Greenwood, and when he found the Lost Buckaroo, they knocked him off."

"Yeah," the little one muttered. "Remember what Perce Robbins said about the samples he assayed for 'em? No wonder he couldn't understand it." Grumpy shook his head soberly. "You had it right when you said we was up against somebody with brains. Blanton's a shrewd article. He musta planned this game out to the letter before he ever hit Wolf River. And how close he came to gittin' away with it!"

"He made just one mistake," said Rip. "He shouldn't have left it to the flood to bury the bodies. If he had attended to it personally, he'd have hit the jackpot."

They waited for Mei-lang and the others to come up. She took the news calmly. Before putting it into Chinese, she asked Rainbow if he were positive that it was Blanton and the alleged prospectors who had killed Moy Kim and Professor Greenwood.

"Absolutely," he told her. "We'll see them go directly to the mine tomorrow. Two of Blanton's party are men who have been working at the Midas Company's mine. They're evidently cut to his pattern, or they wouldn't be with him. I don't believe they had anything to do with the murder."

"What about Wild Bill Melody?" William inquired. "He has always been highly regarded around Wolf River."

"Shucks!" the little one spoke up. "Blanton hired him to make it appear that he didn't know where to find the Lost Buckaroo! Wild Bill is only frontin' for him. If the old boy don't know it by now, he will tomorrow. He's due to find himself in a mighty tough spot, I reckon."

"I'm afraid that's true," Rip agreed. "Having served his purpose, they won't let him go—not with what he knows. You translate, Mei-lang, and we'll go on."

Learning who had killed their countryman aroused the violent wrath of the Chinese. They felt less strongly about Greenwood.

The desert miles were long and seemingly endless. During the afternoon, the wind kicked up again, and presently they were walking into a gray cloud of flying sand that stung their faces and ground into their eyes. Rip arranged a bandanna to protect Mei-lang's face and told her to follow close behind him.

"If the sand gets too bad, we'll stop and turn up the carts for a windbreak."

The sandstorm pelted them for an hour before it passed. There were no tracks to follow now. The sun was in the west already. Grumpy caught Rip glancing at it and read the tall man's thought.

"About two hours of daylight left," he said. "We didn't do so good this afternoon. William, how far do you say we are from Spanish Tanks?"

Chew conferred with Chang before answering.

"We think it's about eight miles, Mr. Gibbs. Chang is going by those two notched peaks you see in the Solomons. It's a landmark."

The mountains looked much nearer than that, but the partners knew distances were deceiving to the eye in the thin, clear air of the high desert.

"We'll go on for another hour before we stop for supper," said Rip. "We'll split up then; you and Grump can head for the Tanks; the rest of us will turn west."

Before the sun sank below the horizon, Rip swept the desert with the glasses, making sure they were alone. Supper followed a few minutes later. Rice, smoked pork, and tea sufficed for the Chinese. The partners pieced it out with a can of beans. As they ate, Rip and Grumpy ran over the way in which matters were to be handled at Spanish Tanks.

"I reckon William and I can take care of it," the little one stated. "We won't walk in blind, tomorrow mornin'; we'll make shore there's no one there."

"And you're to stick until we show up," Rainbow reiterated.

"When do you figger that'll be?"

"By noon, I'd say—if things go our way. But, no matter what happens, I don't want you to come looking for us."

Grumpy wagged his head grimly.

"It ain't goin' to be easy to stay put, once it becomes plain that you've run into trouble. But we will. What do we do if Stewart or that other bunch shows up?"

"I don't believe you'll see anything of them before tomorrow evening," said Rip. "We've taken it out of ourselves, but we've come pretty fast. Chang says it's the best time he's ever made. Of course, if they show up, the only thing you can do is to let them come in. Tell them where they stand, as far as the mine is concerned. If you can get them to throw in with us, okay. I'll leave that to you. But be sure you know who you're doing business with before you give them the word to come in."

The little one dismissed all this advice with a disparaging grunt.

"Don't worry 'bout me! I'll know what I'm drawin' to before I ask for cards!"

Chapter Fifteen

GUN TROUBLE AHEAD

THEY REMAINED WHERE THEY WERE until the afterglow faded into black night. Without any formal leavetaking, Grumpy and young William continued on in the direction of Spanish Tanks. Rip spoke to Chang, and the carts were soon moving toward the base of the mountains.

Mei-lang walked at the tall man's side, her manner sober and constrained.

"I see you're worrying about them," said he.

"Naturally," she admitted. "Grumpy always seems to come through, but William is so young and inexperienced. We Chinese are proud of him, Rainbow. We have so few on whom to pin our hope that some day our people may be treated with respect and dignity."

"He'll be all right," Rip assured her. "Grumpy will see to it. I'm not so sure we won't find ourselves in hot water. I'm counting on Blanton being so eager to reach the mine that he won't have any time to get suspicious."

The blackness faded out of the night as they continued their long detour. With the desert stars bending low to light their way, they swung south along the inhospitable wall of the mountains. Unlike most ranges, the Solomons had no foothills; the transition from the flat floor of the desert to frowning cliffs was immediate.

According to Rip's calculations, they were now about two miles west of Grumpy and William and traveling in a parallel direction. It was after ten o'clock when faint puffs of sound reached them that were unquestionably gunfire. He listened carefully, trying to catch the pattern of the shots.

The shooting was desultory, save for a brief flurry. It continued at uneven intervals for ten to twelve minutes and then stopped as abruptly as it had begun.

"What do you think?" Mei-lang asked anxiously.

"If I read it correctly," he said, "it's worked out exactly as I figured it would. I'm convinced that Blanton thinks he's turned us back. He'll spend an uneasy night at the Tanks. An hour or two before dawn he'll head for the mine."

On reaching the mouth of the canyon, Rainbow asked Mei-lang to speak to Chang.

"I think he understands that what we want to find now —and the sooner the better—is a little cross canyon where we can conceal the carts and ourselves, but I want you to impress it on him. It's almost one o'clock already. And tell Chang to keep in closer to the wall; we're leaving tracks that'll be a complete giveaway if Blanton's bunch happens to spot them."

She addressed herself to Wah Chang at once. Though Rip did not understand a word the man uttered in response, it was plain enough from his gestures that he understood what was wanted. Several times he turned and pointed ahead.

"Chang says we'll find a desirable place within half a mile, Rainbow. He understands he is to lead us in closer to the wall."

The opening into the cross canyon to which Chang led them was so narrow that the carts had to be lifted from the ground a foot or more before they could be put through. Once inside the portal, the defile widened appreciably.

"I couldn't ask for anything better," Rip told Mei-lang. "I'll stay down here until after daylight; I want you and the others to drop back a couple hundred yards. And try to get some sleep; I know you're very tired."

"You'll be safe, alone?" she asked, not trying to conceal her concern.

"Quite," he answered.

"If they pass during the night, will you follow them, Rainbow?"

"No, I'll wait till morning." He smiled at her fondly, longing to take her in his arms again. The memory of a night now long gone, when she had surrendered to his caresses, ran through him like fire.

His thoughts were so close to the surface that she read them easily.

"Good night, my darling," she whispered, so softly he barely heard.

She was gone then. Chang was waiting for her, a few steps away. Rainbow's eyes followed them until a bend in the canyon hid them from view. His eyes were bleak as he turned to begin his long vigil. He knew Mei-lang would disappear from his life again, as she had many times before, and that he would have only the memory of her to sustain him. "Some things become more precious because we know they never can be realized," she once had told him. The tall man recalled the thought and found no consolation in it.

> *East is East, and West is West,*
> *And never the twain shall meet—*

The lines came back to him with a poignancy that bit deeper than usual tonight.

I'll never agree to that, he said to himself. *If I'm beating my head against a stone wall, that's how it will have to be.*

He became so engrossed with his thoughts that the minutes slipped away unnoticed. With a start, he realized that something was moving out in the main canyon. He stiffened to attention, only to discover that it was just a marauding coyote. The animal got his scent and immediately turned tail, stopping every few feet to glance back in Rip's direction and making the night hideous with its barking.

It was not long before the stars began to wink out, and the predawn darkness settled over mountains and desert.

If my timetable is correct, Blanton won't be showing up for another hour, Rip mused. *It should be just about breaking day when they pass here.*

The hour passed without bringing them. The heavens began to grow lighter to the east. Along the horizon, radiating plumes of mauve and rose began to tint the sky. Seen through the iridescent ground mist, which was already beginning to rise, the ever-changing play of colors was unreal and ghostly.

But Rainbow wasn't there to witness the majestic beauty of a desert sunrise. It was growing lighter by the second. Peering through the thinning mist in the direction from which he knew Blanton's party must come, he could see nothing. Suddenly, however, he thought he caught the murmur of voices. He cocked an ear and waited for the sound to come again. He caught it once more, plainer now. In a few seconds, he could make out the wraithlike forms of men. They came closer. He put the glasses on them.

"Blanton!" he jerked out in smothered satisfaction.

"Wild Bill in the lead with the burros and the rest of 'em strung out behind him! All six!"

It meant that Grumpy and William had Spanish Tanks to themselves.

From the course Wild Bill was taking, Rainbow saw that the party would pass within two hundred yards of him. They were hurrying and completely off guard. He put the binoculars on Cord. The latter's face was wolfish in its eagerness. He spoke to Wild Bill every few minutes, apparently urging him to move faster.

When they swung past the defile, they never so much as glanced Rip's way. The tall man kept his eyes riveted on them until they disappeared up the canyon. The sun, a huge golden orb, was peeping over the horizon by now.

"I'll give them three or four minutes before I begin trailing them," he muttered.

Only then did he realize that he wasn't alone. It was Mei-lang. She had been there for some time.

"You saw them?" Rip asked.

"Yes," she murmured tensely. "Must you go alone?"

"I'll be safer that way. You have Chang and the others move up here. See that they keep their guns handy. And whatever you do, Mei-lang, don't leave this spot; you'll be safe as long as your food and water last. Shep Logan and his deputies will be showing up in three to four days."

She winced unconsciously.

"I didn't mean to frighten you," he said reassuringly. "I made it sound more serious than it is. I won't show myself to them if I can help it. I'll be back in less than an hour."

"But you're dealing with desperate men," she insisted, steeling herself against this moment. "They won't hesitate to kill you if they get the chance. Don't be reckless, Rainbow!"

The reserve that seldom failed her snapped without warning, and her arms stole about his neck impulsively. The tall man drew her close and crushed his lips against hers for a long moment.

"Go now," she breathed softly, "and be careful!"

According to William and Chang, the mine was less than a mile and a half from the mouth of the canyon. Rip kept that in mind as he followed the west wall after leaving the defile. He had proceeded only a few hundred yards, when he found the canyon swinging sharply to his right, as it began describing the lower curve of its S shape. It made it impossible for him to see any great distance ahead. He went on carefully for another twenty minutes without catching a glimpse of the six men he was trailing. To his left, the dike became higher. On the other side, the mountain wall, with its crumbling rim, appeared to run along unbroken, but offering few opportunities for scaling it.

From the crest of the dike there was a sheer drop of thirty feet to the rubble that centuries of frost and erosion had tumbled into the canyon. Studying it with the glasses, Rainbow could find no toehold for man or beast. It made him realize how completely the rimrock commanded the canyon.

"I wish I had known more about this setup before we left Wolf River," he said to himself. "I never would have told Logan to wait three or four days before following us in."

Evidence of the cloudburst and resulting flood was still visible. It helped him to put together the story of how Greenwood and Moy Kim had come to their death.

The canyon began to straighten out noticeably. Rip was moving around a huge boulder when he stopped in his tracks. Scarcely two hundred yards ahead of him, Blanton and his men were gathered in an excited ring, with several of them pointing first to the dike and then to the rim.

Rip dropped back and put the glasses on them. It brought them so close that he could catch part of what they were saying by watching the movement of their lips. A pack was opened, and a rucksack was filled with food and ammunition. Then, to Rip's dismay, Blanton ordered Buckout and Kumler to scale the wall and post themselves on the rim, pointing out how they were to reach it. With Wild Bill, Cord and the others then crossed to the dike, where they climbed to a low ledge. There, their excitement increased. Rainbow could see them examining an exposed vein.

"So that's the Lost Buckaroo!" he muttered grimly.

He watched them gloating over their prize for some minutes. An altercation broke out then between Wild Bill and Blanton. The old man's attitude was violently pugnacious. Blanton's manner was even more threatening. Suddenly, a gun appeared in his hand. It had the desired effect, and Wild Bill subsided.

"Mr. Melody knows where he stands now," growled Rip. "God help him if he thinks he can talk himself out of this jam!"

He thought of Logan and his deputies, not due for days.

"No," he decided, "we can't wait; we'll have to handle this ourselves!"

Quickly he made his way back to the defile. Mei-lang and the others saw him coming. He told her what he had seen, and she put it into Chinese.

"Ask Chang if we can reach the rim somewhere along here," he told her. "Everything depends on it, Mei-lang. Pin him down to a definite answer."

She spoke to Wah Chang for several minutes before she turned to Rainbow.

"He says men can reach it but we can't take the carts up."

"That's good enough! We won't need the carts. We'll drop back to Spanish Tanks now and spend the day there. Maybe someone will show up."

"One of the other parties, you mean?"

Rainbow nodded.

"We'll wait as long as tomorrow morning. If we're still alone, we'll go ahead without stalling around for Logan."

They reached the Tanks during the morning. Grumpy came out to meet them. He had a bloodstained rag tied around his head.

"What happened to you?" Rip demanded. "You look a sight."

"A spent slug hit my rifle barrel and reekoshayed! Give me a dang good haircut!" The little one was as full of pepper as ever. "How did things go with you?"

Rip gave him a detailed account of what had happened.

"We could use two or three more men, Grump. We can drive that pair off the rim, once we get up there. Blanton and the rest will run as soon as we do. This is the first place they'll head for. That's all right if we were strong enough to leave three or four men here to grab them."

"Wal, there's somebody up to north of us," the little man declared. "William and me spotted 'em a few minutes ago. Put the glasses on them and see who they are."

The tall man needed no urging.

"It's Tom Stewart! That's a break for us; we know

what we can expect from him. We'll have all the men we need, and to spare."

"Unless we have to chase Blanton and the rest of them skunks all over the map. We want to take 'em alive, don't we?"

"That's the way I hope to take them," the tall man said grimly.

Chapter Sixteen

INTO A KILLER TRAP

"GOOD GRIEF!" TOM STEWART GASPED, pathetic in his amazement as he listened to the story Rainbow unfolded. "I don't know what to make of it, Ripley! It's surprise enough to find you folks here, but what you say about Blanton just about bowls me over."

"Tom, you don't question the truth of what I've told you, do you?"

"No! No!" the mayor exclaimed. "I've made an awful ass of myself!" He shook his head in bitter self-condemnation. "When Blanton showed up in Wolf River, I welcomed him. He had a pretty good reputation around Tonopah. I never tumbled at all when McGarry and Miller showed up with their story of makin' a find. They're squattin' on the mine now, eh?"

"They're there," Rip confirmed. "They went right to it, as I told you."

"Lot of good it'll do 'em!" fat Tom growled. "They'll swing for what they done. Greenwood's daughter will git the Lost Buckaroo. If she's made a deal with Willie and his friends, that's her business." He paused as a new thought struck him, and his surprise turned to anger. "If you knew all this, why didn't you stop me before I came on this wild-goose chase?"

"I'll tell you, Tom," Grumpy put in. "We didn't know but what you was the party we was after. Figger it out for yoreself and you'll see we had to play it the way we did."

"Well, I reckon that's right," Stewart acknowledged, after some thought. "It was a clever game you boys cooked up."

"Did you see anything of Nelson?" the tall man asked.

"Huh, them fools!" Dad Ritchie burst out. "They got lost in Toquima Basin and they'd be there yit if we hadn't come along and straightened 'em out! The last we saw of 'em, they was headin' back to Calamity Creek!"

Dad was fully ten years older than Grumpy, but Rip couldn't help thinking they were cut from the same cloth, sharp-tongued, canny, and tough as bullhide.

Dad eyed Mei-lang with quiet admiration.

"I reckon yo're the first woman ever seen this country," he told her. "It ain't no place for females. It ain't no place for no one but some half-cracked fools. I been right here on this spot when it was so hot yuh thought the gates of hell had opened on yuh."

Before Rainbow got around to it, the mayor volunteered the services of himself and his men.

"We'll see this thing through with you," Tom told him. "We'll go all the way to help you round up them rats. What are your plans?"

"I figured we'd stay here all day and rest," said Rip. "This evening we were going to try and reach the rimrock. I couldn't find any breaks in it. If we're in position to move along it by morning, we can push Blanton's men off. That's certainly the first thing to do. The whole bunch of them will have to run for it then. If we separate them from their burros, they'll be without water. That won't leave them anything to do but head for these springs. We'll have two or three men here to grab them. By then Blanton will know the jig is up. That's the general idea."

Rip turned to Dad Ritchie.

"What do you think of it, Dad?"

"Wal, it's good as far as it goes. We kin git up to the rim all right. I bin up thar. It runs along for 'bout three miles before it pinches out against Sawtooth Peak. That's the big one yuh see off thar to the southwest. But thar's water up that canyon, if they're smart enough to find it. Wild Bill knows about them small springs. But he's a smart old coot. If he was at all suspicious of them fellers, he most likely kept his mouth shet about the springs, figgerin' that would give him an ace in the hole. Give him half a chancst and he'll save his scalp. But yuh got to guard the Tanks. No question 'bout that. The thing to do would be to git them coyotes in between us."

"Can it be done?" Rip inquired.

"Shore it kin! That dike you speak of, it peters out to nuthin'. Go up on the desert side of it and cross over to the wall and yuh can reach the rim. No picnic, I'm tellin' yuh, but yuh can reach it."

"That sounds good, Rip," Grumpy asserted. "We can send a couple men around the dike. There's enough for that; these China boys will give a good account of themselves."

Rip gave it his approval.

"We'll work out the details during the day. I want to send at least two men up the canyon to draw the attention of whoever is on the rim. William and Chang can take care of that. If they run into trouble, we'll be in a position to take a hand. Right now, we'll have something to eat and catch a little sleep. Grump and I have barely closed our eyes for three or four days."

A natural limestone basin, eight feet wide, caught the crystal-clear water that the springs brought to the surface at Spanish Tanks. On all but the hottest days, the flow was heavy enough to cause a slight run-off from the basin, and where the precious water trickled into the sand, there was green grass. A rugged outcropping buttressed the shallow pool on every side, making the Tanks almost impregnable against attack.

The canvas cart covers were set up against the sun. In the tiny squares of shade, Rip and the others slept until early afternoon. When he awoke, he found Mei-lang looking fresh and lovely.

"Hot water does wonders," she answered laughingly, in response to his compliment.

Rainbow ran his hand over the stubble on his chin, saying, "I'll have to try my razor on some of it." He made sure they were alone for the moment. "This may be my only chance to speak to you privately," he continued. "When I said something this morning about sending William and Chang down the canyon, I saw your eyes cloud. They'll be risking their lives. But so will the rest of us. Up on the rim is where I expect the showdown to come. I want William and Chang in the canyon, so they can be the first to reach the mine. William can have the location notices ready. As soon as he reaches the property, have him put the notices in a tin can and put up his monuments. He'll understand that part of it. You explain all this to him. Maybe these precautions aren't necessary, but they'll ward off any chance of an argument. Have I made it all clear to you?"

"Perfectly," she murmured. "You always do what is wise, Rainbow. I'll speak to William later."

In the late afternoon, preparations for supper were begun. Firewood not being procurable, it was necessary to use more of the limited amount of charcoal the Chinese carried in the carts.

When everyone was about to sit down to eat, Dad Ritchie electrified them.

"Somebody showin' up, off thar to the south!" he called out. "Sumthin' familiar about him, to me! Use yore field glasses, Ripley!"

"Looks like Melody," the tall man announced, the glasses to his eyes. He handed them to Dad. "Take a look!"

"Dang my hide if it ain't Wild Bill!" the old man declared. "He's swingin' right along! Just like I told yuh; he slipped the ropes before they got him hogtied!"

He returned the glasses to Rip.

"The rest of yuh go on with yore supper," he said. "Wild Bill and me used to be partners. I'm goin' to walk out and meet him."

The excitement in camp did not subside with his going. The partners made no attempt to conceal their elation at this turn of events. They were moved not only by the fact that Wild Bill somehow had managed to extricate himself from his dangerous dilemma; he was bound to prove a valuable addition to their force.

"He'll have his dander up," Tom Stewart predicted. "And when Wild Bill gits on the prod, he's a fightin' fool."

"He should have some valuable information for us," said Rainbow. "I'm anxious to hear what he has to say."

Fifteen minutes or more passed before the old desert rats walked back into the Tanks. Dad told his old partner who was who. Wild Bill sized up Rip and Grumpy carefully.

"I heard about the two of yuh," he told them. "Comin' from Blanton, it wa'n't a bit complimentary. That damned sidewinder and his gang o' thieves is agoin' to eat lead before I git done with 'em! They was all set to rub me out!"

"We figured they were," Rainbow observed. "I saw Blanton throw a gun on you this morning."

"Oh, did you! Yuh was that close, eh? Wal, they know yo're here; they made a scout along the rim this noon. Blanton's got a pair of four-power glasses. I'm goin' to wet my whistle before I do any more talkin'; I'm a mite thirsty."

"Here's a cup," Grumpy offered. "You don't have to drink outa yore hat, Bill."

The old-timer was too desert-wise to drink his fill at once. After the first cupful, he was ready to talk.

"I began to git wise to what I'd stepped into the night they set the sage afire on yuh, back thar at Picture Rocks. When they wouldn't let yuh git in to water, here at the Tanks, I smelled the rat fer fair. I started figgerin' right then how I was to git outa the mess I was in. It didn't surprise me to have 'em go straight to the Lost Buckaroo. They'd been thar before; they didn't need me to show 'em nuthin'. Them rats killed Henry Greenwood as shore as I'm lookin' at yuh! Has any of yuh seen the mine?"

"William and Chang have," Rip answered.

"Then, Willie, yuh know she's rich. It's goin' to take a heap o' money to develop her. But she's a mine, shore as shootin'!"

"Bill, how did you manage to do a sneak on 'em?" Stewart asked.

Wild Bill laughed thinly.

"I outsmarted the dirty pups! I bin tellin' 'em fer a day or two that yuh couldn't git outa the canyon, 'cept this-a-way. I figgered they'd be needin' water before long.

When they found the bunch of yuh was holdin' down the Tanks, they asked me if I couldn't find some springs. I said I'd try. The fools let me go. I jest went up the canyon to the end of the dike and come down the desert side. Thar used to be water up the other way. Nuthin' thar now. Iffen yuh wanta wait a week, they'll be crawlin' out to yuh with their tongues hangin' out."

"We don't intend to wait," Rip said flatly.

"From what Dad's told me, I figgered yuh didn't. No reason why we should wait; not countin' the young woman, thar's eleven of us. Among us, we kin make them rats hunt their hole. But yo're wrong in figgerin' yuh only got two of 'em to push off the rim; the whole gang's up thar. And that's whar they aim to stick; they know they ain't got a chancst o' holdin' yuh off iffen they make thar fight from the mine."

This was information of the greatest importance, and Rainbow was prompt to say so.

"What have they done with their burros and the rest of their outfit, Bill?" he inquired.

"They cached most of their grub and other gear at the base of the wall. Thar's a little fissure thar. They pushed the animals in with the other stuff and walled it up." Wild Bill chuckled. "Reckon yo're seein' it same as me—git that gang on the run and they won't have no time to pick up thar outfit."

The tall man nodded.

"That's exactly what I'm thinking. There's coffee and hot grub here, Bill. Fill your plate, and we'll talk things over while we're eating."

There were many suggestions as to how best to carry out the attack. In the end, the plan departed only slightly from Rainbow's original proposal. Dad Ritchie was to go down the desert side of the dike and reach the rim below the mine. Bucky Smith and Trammell were to go with him. They were to leave the Tanks as soon as darkness fell. Dad assured Rip that they would be on the rim by daylight, or shortly thereafter.

Four hours after their departure, Rip was to lead his party, consisting of Grumpy, Stewart, Wild Bill, Meilang, and himself to the mouth of the canyon and begin the ascent to the rim. There they were to wait until seven o'clock in the morning before advancing. William and Wah Chang were to leave the Tanks an hour before dawn and make their way into the canyon as far as the defile. At seven o'clock they, too, were to advance. Bow Chee and Gar Lee were to remain at the Tanks, standing guard night and day, until word came from the partners, relieving them.

Since the carts were to be left at the springs, each party had to carry food and water enough to sustain itself.

"We'll take enough to last two days," Rip advised.

"It ain't necessary," Wild Bill argued. "She'll be all over long before that!"

"That's my hunch," the tall man agreed. "But it won't slow us up a bit to play it safe, Bill. Fill the canteens. William and I will parcel out some rations."

After the night had swallowed Dad and his two men, Rainbow waited the four hours that had been agreed on before telling Wild Bill to head for the mountains.

When they reached the wall, the old desert rat led them to the narrow cross canyon where Rip and the Chinese had spent the previous night. At the head of the defile, he pointed out a way to the rim.

"It'll be tough goin', the fust hundred feet," he told them. "Gits easier then. I'll git the little lady up; the rest of yuh'll have to shift fer yoreselves."

Rainbow stayed close behind Mei-lang as they began the ascent. The footing was so treacherous that, even with Wild Bill's assistance and his, she slipped several times.

"Jest keep a-comin', and don't look back," the former advised. "If yuh want to stop to catch yore breath, jest say so. We'll be on the rim in no time."

Rip could hear Tom Stewart panting behind him.

"Can you make it, Tom?" he called back over his shoulder.

"I got a purty big corporation for this sorta thing," Stewart grumbled. "But I'll make it!"

Though the ascent was something less than three hundred feet, it took them an hour and more to reach the top.

"Thar, I told yuh!" Wild Bill crowed. "Nuthin' to it! The quartz is purty rotten along the edge of the rim. Stay away from it."

"Any reason why we shouldn't curl up where we are till daylight, Rip?" the little one demanded, after having a look around. "Seven o'clock is still a long ways away."

"I know it," the tall man returned, "but we'll go on a few yards. We'd be dead ducks if we were caught out here in the open."

"I reckon that's right," Wild Bill declared. "We'll drop back from the rim a ways and hide out behind some rocks. If we git jumped, we kin put up a fight."

Several hundred yards from the lip of the rim, they found great fragments of rock, tossed around in such confusion as to suggest that a race of giants had once been at play there.

Rip selected a spot that offered the necessary protection. He and Grumpy remained awake long after Mei-lang and the others had dozed off. They knew the show-down was near. The moment was not a new one for them, but they were not immune to its tensions. When they finally closed their eyes it was to sleep so lightly that the coming of the sun jerked them awake.

Chapter Seventeen

SHOWDOWN GUNS

RIP ADJUSTED THE GLASSES AT ONCE. After studying the rim for some minutes, he handed the binoculars to the little one. It was a strange world they found spread out before them.

"Looks like the land of the dead," Grumpy muttered. "Ain't even a lizard in sight. How far do you figger we gotta go before we bump into Blanton's gang?"

"A mile—more or less. Looks to me as though we could close in on them without exposing ourselves too much. We'll spread out and move from one rock to the next."

Promptly at seven, they began to advance. Rip kept Mei-lang close to him.

"We'll give them a chance to surrender," he told her, "but I don't expect them to give up without a fight. There's no reason why you should get mixed up in it, accidentally or otherwise. I'll find a safe place for you, and you're to stay there till it's all over."

Mei-lang nodded. Rainbow had seldom spoken to her so brusquely. It gave her an unexpected thrill to have him take charge of her so positively.

They went ahead carefully, their progress limited to a few yards at a time. Wild Bill was on Rip's left; Grumpy moved along at his right. All were so far back from the rim that it was impossible to tell what went on in the canyon. The early morning stillness held, however. Rip used the glasses repeatedly but failed to find any sign of

Blanton and his men. Finally he motioned for Wild Bill to come over to him.

"We're getting close, Bill, but I don't see anything of them."

"They're thar; they ain't cleared out, Ripley. The rim falls away a bit, opposite the mine. It's only a drop of two or three feet, but it goes down in sharp steps. That's why we don't see nuthin' of 'em. We will directly."

They moved on again, but only for a yard or two, when the sharp crack of a rifle knifed through the air. It was followed by three closely bunched shots. A few seconds later, the muffled reports of other guns reached them.

"That's William and Chang!" Grumpy jerked out. "They been spotted! Them first slugs wa'n't directed at us!"

Rip considered it too obvious to require any comment.

A rifle spoke again on the rim. Wild Bill pointed to a tiny puff of white smoke.

"Did yuh catch that, Ripley? The skunks ain't moved a foot from whar they wus when I last saw 'em! We're comin' up in back of 'em jest right! We're shore goin' to give 'em hell!"

"Only as a last resort," Rainbow warned. "You get that straight, Bill. We want those men alive. They get a chance to throw away their guns and surrender."

"Great Christopher!" Wild Bill howled. "That's the fust dumb thing I've heard yuh say, Ripley! Them rats ain't got no idear of surrenderin'! What they got to lose by fightin' it out? Yuh kin only hang a man oncst!"

"They still get their chance," the tall man said flatly. "I've heard outlaws brag that they would never be taken alive. When they found themselves surrounded, they changed their minds in a hurry." He glanced at his watch. "It's a quarter of eight. Dad and his men ought to be all set by now."

"I reckon they're jest waitin' fer us to open up," Wild Bill declared. "Yuh told Dad when he heard our guns talkin' it'd be the signal for his bunch to git busy. A shot or two will start the ball a-rollin'."

"We'll work in a little closer before we fire," Rip announced. After cautioning Mei-lang to remain where she was, he waved Grumpy and the others ahead.

On hands and knees, they advanced another forty yards.

"This is good enough," Rip announced. "Let them know we're here."

The staccato barking of their rifles unleashed an equally sharp blast from Dad and his men. The latter had been in position to close in for half an hour. The thunder of the gunfire rolled over the mountains to lose itself in the far corridors of the Solomons. Down in the canyon, William and Chang let their rifles speak.

"Reckon that gives Blanton some idea of what he's up against!" Grumpy rapped. "They're down on their bellies behind that last step of rock! If they raise their heads, we'll see 'em!"

"Looks like we've got them nailed down," said Rip. "They can't go near the lip of the rim without showing themselves."

Not a shot came from the trapped men. To draw their fire, Grumpy resorted to the old trick of placing his hat on the barrel of his rifle and cautiously raising it above the rock behind which he crouched. Instantly a hornet's nest of slugs whined over his head.

"That stirred 'em up!" the little man chortled. "Ain't much left of that hat."

He glanced at Rip, anxious to know what the next move was to be.

Rainbow's attention was focused on a tangle of rocks ahead of him.

"Why take a chance?" Grumpy demanded fiercely. "They'll cut you down if you try to git up closer!"

"I'll be okay if the three of you will cover me. I can make myself heard on the rim from there. Start throwing lead. Make it so hot for them that they'll have to stay down."

Their rifles began to cough violently. Bent low, Rip raced across the open ground and reached his goal unharmed. Raising his voice, he called on Blanton to surrender.

"Surrender?" Cord yelled back. "Why in hell should we surrender to you? You ain't running us out of the country, Ripley, so you and your Chinks can grab the mine!"

"Forget the mine, Blanton!" Rainbow returned. "We want you, Miller, and McGarry for the murder of Henry Greenwood and Moy Kim! You haven't a chance of holding out! Shep Logan and a posse are closing in on you!" This was for further persuasion. "Throw your guns away and give yourselves up while you're still in one piece!"

"You want us, come and get us!" was Cord's defiant answer.

"All right, Dad!" the tall man yelled. "Let 'em have it!"

It was only a magnificent bluff on his part, but it bore fruit at once. Dad and his two men had been inching toward the rim. From where they lay now, they could see Blanton and his companions flattened out behind a rock parapet. Carrying out Rainbow's instructions, they made their first volley high. Even so, it threw Blanton and his followers into a panic. Their position was exposed now, and the idea seized them at once that they could not remain on the rim and live.

Hank Buckout darted to the edge of the wall and took a downward step, when Grumpy dashed at him, yelling for him to throw up his hands. Instead, Buckout whirled and fired at him point-blank. The slug screeched past the little one's cheek so close that he felt its hot breath. Not trusting a rifle now, he whipped up his .45 and squeezed the trigger. Buckout swayed momentarily and, losing his balance, plunged to the canyon floor.

Rainbow saw Tom Stewart go down. He thought the mayor had stopped a bullet. Tom had only stumbled. Lying in that position, Blanton leveled his rifle at him. Before he could fire, Rip shot the gun out of his hands. The agonized scream that broke from Cord's lips was proof enough that the slug had glanced off the rifle and plowed a deep furrow up his right arm.

By now, Kumler and McGarry were over the rim and picking their way down the wall. Miller started to follow. Wild Bill spun him around with a bullet that struck high on his left shoulder.

Miller had no further use for his rifle. Hurling it at the old man, he followed Pat and Kumler down the wall.

Blanton had drawn a revolver. He slapped a shot at Rainbow and then leaped to the edge of the rim.

"Take another step and I'll drop you!" Rip warned.

For answer, Cord jumped. A ledge ran along the wall, ten feet from the top. He landed on it safely and scrambled to his feet.

"All right, stand where you are!" Rip commanded. "This is your last chance, Blanton! Don't make me kill you! Throw up your hands!"

Grumpy and Wild Bill had the others covered. Kumler knew he had the least to lose by giving up. He raised his hands. McGarry and Miller followed suit.

Cord cursed them viciously. Every vestige of the restraint he had practiced so long was gone now. His face contorted with snarling rage, he looked up along the rim. The number of guns trained on him left him no choice. He dropped his revolver and slowly raised his hands.

Rip ordered the four men to proceed down the wall.

"You and Bill follow them," he told Grumpy. "Keep them covered. If they try to make a break, drop 'em. I'll get Mei-lang. We'll all be down in a few minutes."

He thanked Dad Ritchie for his part in the fight.

"You were right where we needed you, Dad."

"Wal," Dad declared with a chuckle, "yuh know what they say—git thar fustest with the mostest. I figgered I might git a chancst to lift a little hair, but she was all over too quick."

Rainbow had a few moments alone with Mei-lang. It wasn't necessary to tell her how the fight had gone.

"Have you seen anything of William and Chang?" she asked.

"In the excitement, I forgot all about them," he confessed. "I'm sure we'll find them waiting when we get down."

That proved to be the case. The last shot had barely been fired when William and Wah Chang hurried across the canyon to take possession of the mine. William had his notices ready. Building the little rock monuments around them required but a few minutes.

Tom Stewart had preceded Rip and Mei-lang down the wall. Dismissing the prisoners with a glance, he waddled over to the dike to feast his eyes on the richness of the

Lost Buckaroo.

Seeing him there, Rip said, "You better go over, too, Mei-lang. Find out what William proposes to do. He may want to remain here."

"I don't believe so," she told him. "I think he intends to return to Wolf River with us and take care of the legal procedures. Chang and the others will stay, I imagine."

"Talk to him," Rainbow urged. "My idea is to leave here as soon as I can. I'll be over in a few minutes."

He found Dad Ritchie, Bucky Smith, and Trammell gathered about the lifeless body of Hank Buckout.

"What do we do with him, Rip?" Dad asked.

"We'll have to take him in with us. Bill says Blanton hid his burros along here. Have you found them?"

Dad indicated a crack in the wall with a jerk of his head.

"We better git 'em out, I reckon. We'll wrap this fella up and lash him on one of the critters. How soon we movin'?"

"We've got grub and water. We'll have a bite to eat and be on our way."

Grumpy and Wild Bill had the four prisoners herded against the wall. Rainbow walked over to them. Blanton began an abusive tirade at once.

"Break that off where you are," the tall man admonished with chilling finality. "If you're innocent, you'll get a chance to prove it. As for your chatter, I'm not interested. Do your talking to Dennis McCaffery. I'm sure he'll be glad to hear anything you have to say. Bill, see what you can do about his arm. That man's shoulder needs attention, too. We're going to eat before we pull out. That'll give the two of you a chance to have a look at the mine. I'm going over now."

"Say! You were yapping about Logan!" Blanton snarled. "Where is he?"

"He'll find us," Rip said without turning back.

Stewart hailed him as he approached.

"Come up here, Ripley!" he urged. "Take a look at this vein! The Lost Buckaroo wasn't no pipe dream! I reckon I can show you why Johnnie Bidwell couldn't find his way back to it!"

Tom's explanation seemed plausible to Rainbow.

"Course it's plausible!" the mayor insisted. "You can see where that ledge let go. It jutted out above the vein at one time. A 'quake shook it off and dropped it where it is today. I reckon it was years settlin' down that far. When Johnnie came back, his vein was covered." He turned to William. "You're a geologist, Willie, and you say I'm right."

The young Chinese grinned. This was the first time the mayor had ever sought his opinion on anything.

"What I see, Mr. Stewart, compels me to agree with you. Minor earthquakes are not uncommon in this country."

"Those grayish streaks in the vein," Rip queried. "Can it be silver?"

"Of a kind," said William. "It's platinum. If there's any amount of it, we're doubly fortunate." He was obviously overwhelmed by the great opportunity that was now to be his. The moment had its emotional tug for him, too, and he spoke with deep feeling of Professor Greenwood. Humbly he endeavored to express his gratitude for all the partners had done.

"We can skip that," Rip said. "Have you talked things over with Mei-lang?"

"Yes," William replied. "I'll return to Wolf River with

you and do the necessary work at the courthouse. Chang will remain here, and when we reach the Tanks, I'll send Bow Chee and Gar Lee to join him. We'll have to find a way to freight in lumber with which to build a shack, and we'll need timbers and machinery. We can get through Spirit Valley easily enough, but that open country, where we had so much trouble with the arroyos, will give us a lot of bother. Put a road through there and it would be washed out every spring."

"You can keep a trail open, once you git it broken," Stewart observed. "Lord knows you won't have to do any scratchin' for money; you can finance this proposition right in Wolf River."

Rip turned away to study the contour and position of the ledge in relation to the rim where the flight had taken place. Mei-lang moved along with him.

"Is there any doubt in your mind that Professor Greenwood and Kim retreated to this ledge to escape the flood?" she asked.

"None at all. You can see how high the water came. When they were forced to move up this high, they were helpless. Blanton's bunch opened up on them. I know from examining the slug we found in Greenwood's spine that it had traveled at least three hundred yards before striking him. That's about the distance from the ledge to the rim. The bodies toppled into the rushing water and were carried away."

They moved around a shoulder of the ledge and found a shallow indentation.

"Too bad Greenwood and Kim were driven out of here," he remarked soberly. "No one could get at them from the rim."

He was about to step out when he caught the glint of

a rifle cartridge that had been forced into a crack in the rock. It was wedged in so tightly that he had to use his knife to remove it.

"Strange," he muttered. "It was wedged in there for a purpose."

He turned the empty cartridge over in his fingers and was startled to find a tightly rolled piece of paper in the chamber.

"It must be a note!" Mei-lang exclaimed.

She supplied a hairpin, and Rainbow extracted the spindle of paper.

"It is a note!" he told her. "Signed with Greenwood's name!"

This is the Lost Buckaroo. We were fired on last night. Three men on the rim. One of them Blanton, Wolf River saloonkeeper. Cloudburst this morning. Water getting higher. Can't stay here much longer.

"To use your own words, that makes it airtight," said Mei-lang. "Those men can't escape punishment now."

"We didn't need it, but I'm glad to have it just the same," Rainbow declared.

He caught Grumpy's attention and waved him over.

"Take a look at this," he said, after explaining how he had found the note.

"*Jee*rusalem!" the little one jerked out. "That does it, Rip! Not even a McCaffery can bungle this case now!"

They were back at Spanish Tanks two hours later. Stopping only briefly, they continued north. By the next afternoon, they were nearing Picture Rocks. A faint trace of dust on the horizon claimed Grumpy's attention.

"That's men," he said to Rip. "It could be Logan. Put the glasses on them."

"It's Logan, sure enough," the tall man confirmed. "It's a big party. He's got Lane with him, and Blanchard. I swear, there's McCaffery, too!"

"I ain't surprised," the little man declared, with a scornful grunt. "He wa'n't goin' to be left out."

Conversation between them relapsed into a long silence. Grumpy prided himself on being able to read Rainbow's mind, and he knew what his partner was thinking now.

"We won't be around Wolf River much longer," said he. "Three or four days."

"Not that long," Rip monotoned. "I want to get away quicker than that. Grump, anything we've done for Lane Greenwood and Mei-lang had no strings on it. We've paid up some old debts. At least that's the way I feel about it."

"What's this leadin' to?" was the little man's puzzled rejoinder.

"Mei-lang's said something about giving us a piece of the Lost Buckaroo. She and William are going to talk it over with Lane. I don't know how you feel about it, but I don't want any part of it."

Grumpy did not voice his decision at once. It always gave him a wrench to turn his back on anything resembling money.

"Wal," he declared finally, "I reckon if that's the way you feel I'll have to go along with you. But it ain't only their generosity yo're runnin' away from."

"I know it," Rip admitted. "When we were on that case in Star City, I couldn't understand Mei-lang leaving without even saying good-by. I realize now that that's the way to go. It makes it easier for both of us."

"I reckon it does," Grumpy agreed. "But you don't have to tear yoreself apart about it; you'll be seein' her again. When you git back to Wyomin' and git a horse between yore legs once more, you'll be all right."

Rainbow nodded woodenly.

"I guess that's the way to look at it."